FATE IS CURIOUS

ROSIE CHAPEL

First printing 2019

ISBN: 978-0-6485283-4-0

Ulfire Pty. Ltd.

P.O. Box 1481

South Perth

WA 6951

Australia

www.rosiechapel.com

Cover Image: Courtesy Period Images

Cover Designed by Lisa Miller with Got You Covered

❀ Created with Vellum

*To find a second, forever kind of love is a rare gift.
To those who dared to take the risk, who grasped it with both hands,
and cherished it... this book is for you!*

ACKNOWLEDGMENTS

Heartfelt appreciation to Lisa Miller for creating my gorgeous cover.
Special thanks to…
Melanie, for being game enough to read this as a raw and unedited manuscript.
Jackie, for putting up with my nonsense and helping with the final draft.
Amy, for being my sounding board.
Selena, for confirming my French was not as appalling as I thought!

You ladies are awesome!

As ever, grateful thanks to…
Graham at *A Fading Street Publishing Services* for his editing magic, and my hubby for the technical stuff!

CHAPTER 1

Charlotte Hastings, Countess of Sherbrooke, stood on one of the balconies of a graceful four-storey house on the *rue d'Anjou*, just off the *rue du Faubourg Saint Honoré* in Paris. She had been standing there for what seemed an age. When she walked out onto the ornate parapet, the sun had yet to begin its descent to the horizon. Now, it had set, and the dazzling blue of the sky had morphed through a glorious fiery red to a pinkish-grey — the muted hue mirroring her sombre mood.

For, to Charlotte, it was as though everything had stopped. Life would never be the same again.

Oliver, her heart, her soul, her forever — had gone. Just like that, in what felt like the blink of an eye, he was no more. She refused to believe it. One minute he was holding her hand, telling her he loved her, then it was though someone had snuffed out the last candle in the world. The light faded from his eyes, and his hand slipped out of hers to lie, limply, on the sumptuous bed clothes.

She shook her head. Oliver was so... vital. How could he not be alive? How could she go on without him?

One day Oliver was fine. The next, he mentioned his head was throbbing and his throat was scratchy but dismissed both as insignificant. His days were busy and long, especially at the moment while France was transitioning to a new king. A headache was a minor, almost predictable consequence, and naught by which to be alarmed.

Unfortunately, this was far more serious than a mere headache. The following morning, Oliver went to work, and tried to continue as normal, but could not summon up the energy, and the embassy sent him home to rest. That evening, he was wracked with fever. Day and night, Charlotte sat with him, tending to his needs, cooling his hot skin and dosing him with, not only the medications prescribed by the doctor, but also several of her sister-in-law's tried and trusted remedies. The symptoms seemed to ease; Oliver rallied. Then, last afternoon, his condition deteriorated.

Despite Charlotte's diligence, and the efforts of Docteur Allard, the physician assigned to the embassy, Oliver did not respond.

Now he was dead.

Charlotte was frozen. A hard lump had settled where her heart used to be. She had no idea what to do. Their two children had yet to be told. They knew their Papa was unwell, but everyone was confident he would be up and about by week's end. Charlotte was aware, if she cried, it might help, might alleviate the pain, but she had no tears.

There was much to do… no… none of that mattered today. Today, what was left of it, was for her children, everyone else could wait. Pulling herself together, Charlotte turned away from the spectacular view over the roofs of Paris, a view she barely registered, and retraced her steps across their bedchamber.

Their bedchamber, it was no longer *theirs*, it was hers. Charlotte slumped onto the chair positioned beside the bed, where Oliver lay so still — almost as though in a deep sleep. His body would need to be prepared, but this was France and she was not cognisant of the rules — that Oliver would die on foreign shores never occurred to either of them. She wanted to take him home to Sherbrooke, their country estate, where he could be buried in the family plot, but was unsure whether transporting a body was permitted or even appropriate. The alternative, to leave him in Paris, among strangers — unconscionable.

Charlotte heaved a sigh and took Oliver's hand. It was cold, but she didn't care. Lifting it, she kissed his knuckles, then held it against her face.

"What do I do? Oliver, what do I do? You weren't supposed to die, to leave me here, alone. How do I go on without you?"

Oliver, of course, didn't respond, but Charlotte could hear his voice in her head.

Charlotte my darling, one thing at a time. First, you must tell the children. They do not need to hear of this from the staff. Noah will try to be brave. I doubt Millie will really understand. I know it will be hard, to explain why I can't play with them anymore, but please just tell them the truth. Don't prevaricate. Children are canny little souls; they know when we are not being honest.

Then write to your mother. I know she will want to be with you, to help you... let her. Permit Donaldson to take care of the rest. Spend time with the children, go for walks, savour the last breath of summer.

Charlotte, I love you. I'm sorry I left you, but please do not waste your life mourning me. Embrace every single moment. I'll find you again... eventually.

Charlotte stretched up and kissed Oliver's cheek. "I'll try my love,

I'll try." She leaned back, placed his hand on the bed and patted it, brushing over his long, slender fingers. She always thought Oliver had artist's hands; hands which, with a simple touch, could calm her or transport her to the heights of bliss. No more.

Standing, she straightened the bed clothes, and stared at her husband for a long moment.

Then, she left the room, closed the door, and went to find Noah and Millie.

~

The next two weeks passed in a blur. Everything continued around Charlotte, but nothing touched her. Letters were sent to a variety of people. Oliver's secretary and man of business, the aforementioned Donaldson, handled most of them, but Charlotte wrote to her family. Oliver's parents were dead, and he had no siblings, a blessing she did not appreciate until this moment.

Then there was the house, this beautiful house in the centre of Paris where they had been living for the last two years. Rather than rent somewhere, Oliver bought this property, arguing it gave them a home in Paris, even after his appointment with the British Embassy came to an end. It was a decision neither regretted. They loved the city and were part of a small but close-knit group of friends. Noah, and Millicent — known to all and sundry as Millie — were happy, they had several playmates, and Noah was looking forward to beginning lessons with some of his friends.

Until Oliver's death they had no plans to return to England. Charlotte wasn't ready to leave Paris, *but* she wasn't sure she wanted to bury Oliver here.

In the event, Charlotte arranged for Oliver to be interred at the recently opened *Cimetière des Grandes Carrières* in Montmartre, the eighteenth arrondissement of Paris, and not too far from their home. She did not think it sensible to delay the burial, not least because she had no mind to witness her beloved husband's body begin to decay. The temporary grave marker would be replaced by a tombstone more suited to Oliver's status as soon as it was finished.

The enormity of his loss and the changes it wrought on their lives threatened to overwhelm Charlotte. Her mind refused to settle, questions without answers swirled around her head in chaotic abundance. She lost her appetite and found sleep eluded her. Noah and Millie kept her sane. With the resilience of youth, they cried, talked about what had happened, and moved on.

Seven-year-old Noah understood more than his sister, who had just turned four, although neither of them appeared to be swamped by grief, for which Charlotte was relieved. She had yet to weep for the loss of her husband. She knew she ought to, but was afraid, if she gave in to tears, she would never stop. Thus, even though her control was hanging by the slenderest of threads, she bit her lip... figuratively speaking... and carried on with life as though all was normal.

Her friends were solicitous and, while offering support, were not suffocating in their compassion. Charlotte was appreciative of their sensitivity; it was all she could do to drag herself out of bed each day — to welcome numerous, well-intentioned, callers was beyond her. Thankfully, being in mourning meant she could avoid all formal engagements for at least six weeks, longer if she felt it appropriate. Charlotte was unsure she would ever attend another ball or soiree again — to go without Oliver? Unthinkable.

Twelve days later, Charlotte was sitting in the garden, watching Noah and Millie, who were playing with two kittens, offspring of the kitchen cat. Their antics were amusing, and Charlotte was amazed to discover she could still smile. It was mild for October, and Charlotte wanted her children to enjoy as much fresh air as possible. Too soon it would be winter, and outdoor pursuits would be curtailed. Masson, the butler, came to ask whether she was receiving visitors. Charlotte was about to shake her head when Masson murmured something only she could hear.

Charlotte's mouth fell open.

"Are you sure?" she whispered, not quite believing what he said.

Masson nodded. "*Oui*, my Lady."

Charlotte stood on suddenly unsteady legs and turned to watch as the butler escorted three ladies and one gentleman into the garden. Charlotte did not recognise the latter, but the trio were dearly familiar. Of their own volition her arms lifted, reaching for the oldest of the three.

"Mama," it was a sad lament. The woman enfolded Charlotte in her arms.

"Oh, my poor child."

Finally, the tears flowed.

CHAPTER 2

The gentleman who accompanied the women into the house felt more than a little awkward witnessing such all-consuming sorrow. He should not be here; this was a time for family. He said as much when they alighted moments ago, only to be assured, after all he done for them during the last few days, he would be welcome at the Sherbrookes' home.

Tall, and tanned, his long, dark-brown hair — threaded with a trace of grey — caught back in a queue, Zacharie Romain was the owner of the ship which carried the three ladies and their, surprisingly limited, retinue from the Port of London to Calais. Upon disembarking, his fleet of carriages transported them from the coast to Paris. During the journey, he learned much about the woman they were coming to see and, although all were patently devastated by the loss of Lord Sherbrooke, their concern, understandably, was for his widow.

Zacharie empathised. He was not untouched by loss. His work was perilous. Death at sea was not unusual, he had been on ships when sailors perished from illness or misadventure. Moreover, his wife, Nathalie, had died in childbirth, and although this was over a decade previously, Zacharie's sorrow lingered. Not the type to frequent brothels, you could catch your death there…

literally… Zacharie was resigned to a celibate life — he had never met anyone who came close to evoking the same emotions as had Nathalie.

Zacharie observed the women as they took control. Lady Helena and the younger Lady Winchester gathered up the two children and whisked them into the house distracting them with talk of hot chocolate and cakes while the dowager countess virtually carried her daughter to a wrought iron bench. Lady Sherbrooke's sobs were wretched, and she didn't seem able to curb her tears. Zacharie was torn. Although unwilling to interrupt this family reunion, he wanted to leave — at the same time accepting it was impolite to do so without saying goodbye, especially after their insistence he come in with them.

He backtracked to the doorway, wondering whether either of the younger ladies was close by. He could hear laughter, and the high-pitched tones of young children chattering nineteen to the dozen. It was coming from what he guessed to be the direction of the kitchens. A grudging smile tugged at his lips; these ladies were a most unusual trio. They were nothing like those of the nobility he usually ferried across the channel. They had travelled with little luggage, meagre staff and all wore sensible clothing — suited to long journeys and inclement weather. Practical rather than frivolous.

He now knew Lady Helena and Lady Augusta, were sister and mother to Lady Sherbrooke, respectively. Billie, as Lady Winchester demanded he call her, despite his attempts to use her title — was married to Lady Augusta's son, Giles — the current Earl of Winchester. The familial connection between Lady Sherbrooke, her sister, and her mother was unmistakeable. All three were of average height, raven haired — the dowager's sprinkled with white — and similarly featured.

Billie, on the other hand, was petite, with chestnut hair and shrewd green eyes. Her slight stature, however, concealed a spirited personality and, as Zacharie had occasion to witness during the journey, someone who did not suffer fools gladly. In fact, none of the women he had escorted to Paris were the shrinking violet types — a rather exasperating characteristic and one which, in his experience, was peculiar to Society ladies. His passengers were interesting, witty, forthright, and — in the nicest possible way — unapologetically opinionated. Women who could hold an intelligent conversation about a variety of topics, whom, he surmised, would go out of their way to support and protect those they cared about. The sort of women who commanded respect. A slightly cynical ship owner, and long-time sea-captain, Zacharie found their candour refreshing, their company exhilarating and... he admitted to himself... was honoured to be acquainted with them.

While all this was running through his head, Zacharie found his gaze drifting to Lady Sherbrooke. Taller than her sister, she was pale with dark circles under her eyes, which was to be expected, given the circumstances. Her plain gown was in the drab black bombazine associated with bereavement, her glossy hair pulled back into a neat bun, and he noted, absently, the severe style suited her.

There was no doubt the countess was a beautiful woman and — even acknowledging how inappropriate it was, she was a grieving widow for goodness sake — dammit if his body didn't agree with his mind.

Zacharie turned, about to make his excuses, he was correct in his assertion he should not be here, when he heard an odd sound from the direction of the bench. He spun back and, meeting Lady Augusta's concerned gaze, hurried over.

"Is there something you need, my lady?" he asked.

Lady Augusta inclined her head towards the woman who was now resting against her shoulder. "My daughter has cried herself to sleep. I know this is not part of your purview, and my request may be deemed improper, but might you be so kind as to..." she paused, a hint of a frown creased her brow, clearly uncertain how to phrase her petition without offending him.

In quick understanding, Zacharie scooped Lady Sherbrooke into his arms and followed her mother into the cool of the house. Up two flights of stairs and along a maze of corridors, footsteps silent on the thick carpet, Zacharie conveyed his burden; one, he noted, who seemed far too light for her stature. Finally, they came to a door, which Lady Augusta pushed open, and then stood aside allowing him to precede her into the bedchamber.

It was a room which, Zacharie believed — even though he had yet to be introduced to the woman he was carrying — reflected her. Understated elegance was the best term he could come up with. The quality of the furnishings was obvious, but they were not overly lavish, in fact, some looked well-worn and very comfortable. He laid Charlotte carefully into the crisp white sheets, fighting an urge to smooth stray wisps of hair off her tear-stained face. She looked unutterably fragile.

"Thank you, Zacharie." Lady Augusta's calm voice broke through his reverie. "Please would you be so kind as to ask Billie to join me. I think we have need of her tinctures."

"My pleasure, my lady. I shall take my leave, if you have no objection. This is a time for family. Should you require my services while you are here, please do not hesitate to send for me. I have business in Dieppe requiring my attention and will not be sailing to England until you are ready to return. Thus, I am at your disposal." He bowed and left the room.

Augusta Winchester watched Zacharie depart. He was a revelation. Hugh Drummond, Helena's husband, owned Trentams — a prosperous shipping company — and Augusta had presumed it would be one of his ships on which they traversed the Channel. Unfortunately, his fleet was either at sea or under repair and, although several were due to dock within a week, none who were travelling wanted to delay unless they had no alternative.

Hugh recommended Romains, Zacharie's family-owned business, and it was Hugh who asked whether his friend had any available vessels. Romains was a fledgling company compared with Trentams, but Zacharie's reputation was unblemished and, if Hugh trusted his wife's safety to one of Zacharie's ships, that was all the assurance Augusta required. Sea travel was not without its hazards, and, of the three, only Billie had been on board a ship, for more than a tour of the vessel, prior to this voyage. Not that any would have known it, they all appeared exhilarated, spending most of the crossing on deck.

Making a mental note to invite Zacharie to dinner while they were in Paris, Augusta turned her attention to her daughter.

Under the loving care of her family, Charlotte was coaxed into eating regular meals and — aided by Billie's famous brews — began to sleep through the night. As the weeks slipped by, she lost her waif-like appearance and her skin was restored to its usual healthy radiance.

Zacharie Romain became a sporadic visitor. Once Charlotte was feeling more sociable, her mother decided it was *imperative* she be shown every square foot of the city and availed herself of Zacharie's offer to assist in that endeavour. That this was a ruse by Lady Augusta to encourage Charlotte to live again never crossed the latter's mind. Lady Augusta, however wanted to be sure her daughter would not revert to her hermit-like existence, the minute they departed.

Zacharie proved an amusing and entertaining companion and guide. He knew Paris well, and often took them to places most visitors would never think to explore. Weather permitting, he also seized every opportunity to go beyond the city and into the countryside. These were the days when Charlotte thrived. The endless vistas, painted in autumnal shades of bronze, purple, red and gold, were a balm to her bruised heart.

CHAPTER 3

$\mathcal{W}$inter loomed, and none wanted to be caught in the severe weather which stalked the English Channel at this time of the year. Helena and Billie had their own lives — husbands and children whom they missed and who in turn missed them — if the mountain of correspondence was any indicator. Charlotte's mother, widowed for a decade, had nothing in London demanding her attention and was pondering whether to extend her visit until the spring.

One evening over dinner, about six weeks after their arrival, Augusta — in a roundabout way — broached the subject.

"I do believe 'tis nearing time for us to return to England. We do not wish to overstay our welcome and it would be prudent to leave before we are unable to do so owing to the weather."

There was a brief silence, then Billie spoke.

"Despite the gravity behind our visit, this has been, for the most part, a wonderful sojourn. To spend time with you," she nodded at Charlotte, "and your adorable children has been a boon. I confess, however, I find my thoughts winging to Whiteoaks." She did not add being away from her husband and children left her feeling less than whole — that would be insensitive, and, in any case, all at the table knew the depth of affection each bore for their respective families.

"My dears," Charlotte observed, with a smile, "you have been more than generous with your time. That you came at all was a blessing I did not anticipate. You have rescued me, truly. I could not see any way out of the pit of despair I had fallen into, yet your love, compassion, and dogged determination not to let me wallow in my grief has warmed my empty soul and lifted my spirits. Thank you from the bottom of my heart."

"If you are agreeable, I should like to stay a little longer, perhaps until the spring." Augusta interjected, almost apologetically. The other three stared at her. None had any idea she was even contemplating a delay in her return to England. Under their shocked scrutiny, Augusta felt an uncharacteristic blush wash up her cheeks. "I have nothing pressing at home. Yes, it will mean amending my plans for Christmas but, if I am not imposing, I believe my presence could be beneficial." Then she stopped being formal and added. "I miss you, Charlotte. Until this month, I have barely seen you since your marriage. While I accept this is as it should be, mayhap we have been granted an opportunity to enjoy each other's company without being hindered by time."

Charlotte, who had been dreading the day her family departed, felt a broad smile begin to curve her lips. "Mama, are you sure? I can think of nothing I would like more. These last few weeks have made me realise how much I miss you, all of you. I admit, I am not ready to say goodbye to Paris, especially as Oliver will remain here, but I was torn. To be close to family means leaving Oliver, to stay near Oliver means letting you go. Mama, thank you, you are welcome to stay as long as you like."

The four women fell to discussing their plans and the rest of the evening flew by.

A missive was dispatched to Zacharie Romain, who called at *Maison de Sherbrooke* at his earliest convenience, and affirmed his ship was available whenever it was required. All he had to do was alert his crew. It was agreed, Helena, Billie, and their staff, would depart Paris early morning this coming Thursday, meaning — weather and tides permitting — they should be in England by Sunday.

Charlotte's spacious home, already bustling with extra numbers, became a veritable hive of activity and, four days later, three coaches rolled up. Farewells were said, hugs shared — the Winchester family were great huggers — assurances of letters to be written, and then they were gone. Before the travellers rattled off down the street, Zacharie took pains to assure Charlotte and Augusta, he would send confirmation of Helena and Billie's safe arrival.

The house on *rue d'Anjou,* seemed unnaturally silent. For nigh on two months, it had been full of laughter and chatter and, although only a few had departed, it was as though they had taken the happiness with them. This was not true, of course, but it took several days for those remaining to adjust. Gradually, life resumed its gentle rhythm. It grew colder, and the household often woke to frost-coated windows, Noah and Millie rushing to trace the fern-like patterns, before they melted under the weak sunshine.

December was upon them, soon it would be Christmas, and while Charlotte had little desire to celebrate, she had no mind to let her children miss any of the festivities. Oliver loved Christmas and always ensured it was a season of joy. He would be upset at the thought of them moping about in a dark, sombre house. It had become a tradition to gather all manner of greenery to decorate their home, and to be embellished with colourful ribbons. There was always a sprig of mistletoe, under which Oliver kissed his wife with flattering frequency. However difficult she found it, Charlotte would honour Oliver by making this a Christmas to remember.

A week slid by, then another, then one bitterly cold afternoon in the middle of December, the peace enveloping *Maison de Sherbrooke* was disturbed by a loud rapping. Opening the front door, Masson was not unduly surprised to see Zacharie Romain on the step. The tall, shipping merchant was carrying a pile of packages in one arm while brushing a faint dusting of snow off his charcoal greatcoat with the other.

"Monsieur Romain, welcome. Come in, sir. How goes the shipping trade?" Masson enquired, politely.

"It goes well, thank you, *monsieur*," Zacharie replied. "Pray tell, are either of the two ladies receiving callers? I have messages and parcels galore from England."

"I am sure they would be delighted to see you. This way, sir." Masson relieved Zacharie of his bundle and ushered him into a room adjacent to the hall. "Please take a seat. I will let Lady Sherbrooke know you are here." Bowing, the butler retreated.

A fire crackled in the grate. Zacharie took advantage of it, and stood with his back to the flames, the heat taking the chill from his body. He had ridden hard from Dieppe and, after arriving in the city, stopped at his lodgings long enough to wash, and change into fresh clothes. Travel at this time of the year was fraught with risk, and his return from England was delayed by wild storms. Three days ago, they finally blew out, leaving the Channel relatively calm once more. His word given, Zacharie hastened to Paris to apprise the Sherbrooke household that the two ladies and their entourage, under his protection were safely home. He studiously ignored the persistent voice inside his head reminding him it also afforded another opportunity to see Lady Charlotte.

CHAPTER 4

Scant moments passed before Masson returned and escorted Zacharie upstairs to the drawing room. This was one of the most eclectic rooms he had ever been privileged to be invited into. Light and airy, the room was charmingly appointed, a subtle blend of the formal and the casual, creating a relaxed ambience. The conservatively styled furniture was adorned with colourful cushions. Subdued window dressings were enlivened by richly patterned brocade sashes. Children's toys were scattered around the floor, one or two books were piled haphazardly on a stool or side-table, and an inkwell stood alongside a sheaf of paper on an escritoire. It was a comfortable room, one where a family lived, worked, and played.

Lit by a multitude of candles, and warmed by a roaring fire, it was also a room with which Zacharie had become familiar while acting as guide to the countess and her visitors. He knew the position of every piece of furniture, that the floor to ceiling windows to his right overlooked the well-maintained garden, and who was depicted in each of the portraits hanging on the wall.

Charlotte rose from her chair by the hearth, greeting Zacharie with a smile. "M Romain, how good of you to call. I trust you are well?"

Zacharie bowed over Charlotte's hand. "I am, indeed, Lady Sherbrooke, thank you for asking. As promised, I come to advise, Lady Helena and Lady Winchester are safely home. I also bear seasonal tidings in the shape of letters, and gifts — the latter now in the charge of Monsieur Masson."

"Tsk, we have only just parted. My apologies, sir, you have enough to contend with on your journeys without the extra burden of frivolities." A glimmer of pink swept up Charlotte's face.

"Do not think on it. I was glad to be of service. Besides, it has been refreshing, spending time with ladies who are not afraid to demonstrate their intellect, and worth any amount of frivolity." Zacharie allowed himself a reminiscent grin, recalling their lively debates while travelling.

Charlotte, conscious of Helena and Billie's blithe disregard for etiquette, responded in kind, commenting. "I am sure they kept you on your toes. Please sit and share any news you may have. Would you care for a drink? Whisky perhaps or would you prefer brandy? Maybe a coffee or hot chocolate?"

Zacharie opted for a brandy, interested to note Charlotte served it herself rather than ring for a footman.

She caught his quizzical expression and chuckled. "I am not so helpless I cannot pour a drink. I like being a little self-sufficient. Papa taught us all to appreciate the assistance provided by our staff, but not to waste their talents by expecting them to under-take minor tasks we... I... am eminently capable of completing. Oliver engaged the requisite staff necessary to keep a home of this size running smoothly, but both he and I shoulder our share, and we want our children to do the same."

There was a clinking sound. Glancing up, Zacharie noticed Lady Sherbrooke's hands were trembling as she placed three crystal tumblers on a small tray, simultaneously registering that she spoke of Oliver as though he was still alive. She covered it with poise but mention of her husband even as an aside was apparently an effort. He reminded himself, it was less than three months since the earl's passing and, from snippets of conversation, Zacharie knew it had been a love match.

"Mama will doubtless join us momentarily," Charlotte continued, a trifle over-brightly, "she is with the children, but Masson will have informed her of your arrival."

They chatted about nothing of any substance and, shortly thereafter, Augusta came into the room. Zacharie handed over the collection of letters entrusted to him by Hugh Drummond and, finishing his drink, made to leave.

"Oh, please, do stay for dinner," Charlotte entreated. "You have been so generous, 'tis the least we can do. I know Noah will be anxious to see you."

The little boy had become quite attached to Zacharie, who could be relied upon to tell wondrous tales of ocean voyages whenever asked. Noah missed his father dreadfully, but all his friends insisted he was now the man of the house, the new earl with innumerable responsibilities, and he needed to be strong for his mother. Thus, Noah had banked down a grief he could scarcely comprehend and tried to be stalwart but always felt relieved when Zacharie was around. It meant he could take a step back and let the Frenchman shoulder some of the burden, if only briefly. Regrettably, Charlotte knew nothing of this, for she would have set her son straight in short order. It would take another year and another shock before she discovered the truth.

"If you are sure I am not imposing, I should be glad to," Zacharie replied, and resumed his seat. The talk went back and forth; a little gossip, and news from the family, which inevitably brought them around to Christmas.

"What of your family, Zacharie?" Augusta enquired.

"'Tis only I." Zacharie shrugged nonchalantly. "I do not celebrate." His rather abrupt reply was softened by his smile, but both women perceived a sadness lurking behind his words. Charlotte made a decision.

"Mayhap you might consider coming here on Christmas

morn?" she invited quietly. "This year will be hard enough. Please..." when Zacharie started to interrupt, she assumed to reject her offer. "...you would be doing me a favour. Even with Mama here, I daresay I shall struggle to maintain a cheerful demeanour throughout the day. Christmas should not be a time for sadness. Were we among family and friends in London, or perhaps Whiteoaks, my melancholy would go unnoticed, but we are not. My children need stability, to be reassured that, despite the loss of their father, their routine will not alter markedly. It is unfortunate his death came so close to Christmas, a day he ensured was full of love and laughter, but 'tis all the more reason to make it as memorable this year as it always has been."

Charlotte held Zacharie's gaze while she spoke, her grey eyes boring into his. It crossed her mind that *his* eyes were a curious shade, almost forest green... dark, fathomless... quite fascinating. A vaguely disconcerting sensation fluttered at the periphery of her mind, gone so quickly she presumed it was a flight of fancy. Mentally, she shook herself, banishing unsettling thoughts — *goodness, what was wrong with her? Her husband was barely cold in his grave.*

Unaware of her daughter's wayward musings, Augusta added her agreement, remarking that they would welcome his presence, and surely, he did not want to spend the day alone?

Zacharie, who along with Charlotte, had detected a corresponding shift in consciousness, hesitated. Something, wholly inexplicable was stirring and, although he could not grasp its significance, was astute enough to recognise it only occurred when he was near Lady Sherbrooke. He needed to remain detached, to avoid situations like this — to hope it could be otherwise was futile. Since Nathalie's death, Zacharie had closed his heart. No one should endure that much agony more than once in a lifetime. He would remain unattached. Now, it seemed this fragile widow had touched something inside him. To spend time in her company would be like rubbing salt into wounds. Yet, despite all good arguments to the contrary, and even as his head declined their invitation, he heard himself accept.

Merde.

CHAPTER 5

Snow fell on Christmas Eve. The grey gloom of the day did not lift, and the streets of Paris were quickly blanketed in white, muffling all sound. Charlotte, Augusta, and the children did not really notice, engrossed in putting the finishing touches to the decorations, and ensuring everything was ready for the following day.

Throughout the previous week, they had gathered armfuls of evergreens. Boughs of laurel, interspersed with sprigs of rosemary, holly laden with berries, and the odd rosy apple, now festooned every mantel, sideboard, and shelf — even the domestic quarters and bedchambers did not escape. Garlands of pine and ivy twisted together with hellebore were woven around the balustrades of each staircase, the white of the Christmas rose, providing a stunning contrast to the darker green. Charlotte and Augusta had fashioned red, silver and gold bows from pieces of ribbon, which Noah and Millie scattered randomly among the greenery. *Maison de Sherbrooke* was nearly ready for Christmas.

The final touch was a mistletoe ball suspended under the huge chandelier in the entrance hall. Every time they passed under it, Charlotte kissed her children, making them chortle with laughter

A small pile of parcels appeared, as if by magic, arranged

neatly on the top of one of the sideboards in the drawing room, behind the decorations and nicely out of reach of little hands. During the year, after the children were in bed, Charlotte had sewn a variety of velvet bags in assorted colours and sizes, the loose material disguising the treasures secreted inside.

Included among this trove were gifts for the staff and a token for Zacharie.

Until three days ago, Charlotte was stumped as to whether it was appropriate to buy Zacharie a gift, his connection to the Sherbrookes being somewhat indiscernible. He was not family, but he had been a great support; he was more than an acquaintance, possibly a friend, but was not, and probably never would be, a regular part of their lives. In the end she chose a silk cravat in the same hue as his eyes. Not overly personal but definitely thoughtful.

Satisfied with their efforts, and before they sat down for dinner, Charlotte asked Noah to light the Yule candle. She had been undecided — observing this tradition would serve as a reminder Oliver was not among them but, in the end, felt it would be worse if they didn't.

The next day, although quieter than previous Christmases, still retained familiar cheer. After breakfast, Millie was asked to blow out the candle, an honour she took seriously. Then they rushed upstairs to be hustled into warm coats, boots, mittens and hats. Once ready, the family — and any staff who wished to join them — trudged the short distance, through thick snow, to the chapel attached to the embassy.

The snow had stopped falling sometime during the night, the temperatures plummeting. Despite the frigid weather, the streets of Paris were bustling. Voices carried on the still air, sounds of children laughing, the jangle of reins and rumble of coaches. When they came out of the chapel, Charlotte blinked back a rush of tears, knowing how much Oliver would have loved being witness to the magical scene in front of her, created by vivid splashes of colour against the silver and white background.

Augusta, sensitive to her daughter's state of mind, appeared by her elbow and chattered away about matters practical, until Charlotte regained her composure.

Zacharie, as instructed, arrived at midday, bearing yet another heap of parcels — it seemed his lot in life was to act as postman. Masson showed him into the drawing room, where he barely had chance to greet the adults, before Noah and Millie swarmed all over him, begging to know what he carried. Zacharie refused to be drawn.

"Ahhh… you must be patient. A large part of the excitement in receiving a gift is the anticipation. Of guessing what it might be. Once you have opened it, *poof…*" he made an exploding gesture with his hands, "… the mystery is solved."

At Charlotte's direction, Zacharie added what he had brought to the pile on the sideboard, then accepted a glass of whisky and took a seat in one of the wing-backed chairs arranged around the hearth. While they made polite conversation, he found himself studying Charlotte. She was wearing a velvet gown, so dark red it was almost black — perchance a nod, both to the season and the fact she was still in mourning. Around her shoulders a fine wool shawl in black, but with a hint of the same deep red at the fringe. Her hair was arranged in a deceptively modest bun, a blood-red velvet ribbon woven through it. In his humble opinion, she was still too pale, but he perceived her eyes were less shadowed.

Charlotte had explained to Zacharie, when he accepted her invitation to spend Christmas Day with them that, rather than wait until the evening, she preferred to have Christmas dinner in the early afternoon. In part, this meant the children would have digested their meal long before they went to bed, but in the main it was because it afforded any staff who wanted to, the chance to visit their own families for the evening.

Neither did the Sherbrookes indulge in numerous courses of overly rich food. This year it would be roast goose with all the trimmings, followed by sweet mince pies, and plum pudding. Three courses were quite enough. The delicious smell of cooking wafted through the house every time the baize door swung open, making stomachs growl.

Before the food was served, everyone in the household gathered in the drawing room when, under Charlotte's watchful eye, the two children distributed the gifts among the staff. Noah carefully read out the name on the tag while Millie handed it to the recipient.

The family's gifts would be held until after the meal.

Then it was time to eat.

One thing Charlotte and Oliver always encouraged was family discussions at mealtimes. It was often the only chance Oliver had during his busy day to hear what his wife and children got up to. All too frequently, he was required to return to the embassy during the evening. This was a habit Charlotte was resolved not to let slide. Thus, while they ate their dinner and then later, when the children were distracted by their new toys, Charlotte learned quite a lot about Monsieur Zacharie Romain. Augusta knew some but not all, and Zacharie had to admit he was flattered by their attention.

It transpired Zacharie had an aunt who resided, with her titled English husband, in Dorchester. At the beginning of the Napoleonic Wars, Zacharie was sent to live with them. He was educated at Eton, then went on to Oxford, where he studied languages and the classics. Despite his nationality, Zacharie's flair for languages came to the attention of the powers that be, and he spent the last few years of the conflict working for the English government. This ability came to the fore again when, after the war ended, he took control of his father's shipping company in Dieppe, upon the latter's untimely demise.

Five years previously, an acquaintance from his university days, who happened to own a shipping company, informed him of the pending sale of a neglected business. It offered a base on the Thames, and Zacharie jumped at it. It took almost a year to restore and refurbish the ageing shipyard, but since then it had flourished. He no longer wasted precious days loitering in the Pool of London, either unloading his cargo onto lighters, or waiting until he was able to dock at the appropriate wharf. The goods in which he traded complemented those of his friend, and they regularly worked together. So frequently, in fact, they were now in talks to amalgamate the two companies and become a single entity.

Coincidentally, this friend was Charlotte's brother-in-law, and the person who recommended Zacharie's company when her family needed to travel urgently. If Hugh Drummond trusted his beloved wife to Zacharie's care, Charlotte knew he was a man who was eminently honest and reliable — someone you could call on in an emergency.

She was also keenly aware Zacharie never spoke of his personal life. She respected his privacy but speculated on it from time to time. He was such a gentleman; any woman would be lucky to have him as their husband.

CHAPTER 6

JANUARY 1827

Charlotte Hastings, Lady Sherbrooke was sitting in the drawing room, trying to re-attach the head onto one of Millie's dolls. She had no idea how the decapitation had occurred but speculated Noah might have been involved. One more stitch, and she was satisfied it was as secure as she could make it. She held it away, tilting her head this way and that, scrutinising her efforts. Regrettably, the doll did rather resemble the image in Charlotte's head of the main character from a book she had read recently, about a creature who was 'made' in an attic. It was a rather distressing tale, truth be told, and Charlotte was thankful her daughter was much too young to be aware of it, and thus would not associate her doll with the hapless creature.

Task accomplished, Charlotte leaned back against the chair, and rolled her aching shoulders, relishing the quiet. Her thoughts, as they did frequently of late, strayed to her son, and Charlotte brooded over the problem of Noah. Since Augusta's departure, almost a year ago, Noah's behaviour had become increasing volatile, his fiery temper, so like her own, almost uncontrollable. It did not seem to matter how she dealt with his outbursts, nothing worked. Unwilling to seem harsh, he was just a child, and Charlotte believed you won more battles with honey than with vinegar, she had tried the gentle approach, to no avail. Eventually, she resorted to moderate punishments, such as confining him to his room without dinner, restricting the hours he played with his friends, removing his favourite toys, even threatening to withdraw him from the school he attended. Noah adored school; he was an intelligent boy and soaked up his lessons like the dry earth soaks up rain. None had any effect, and Charlotte was at a loss.

In the quiet of the afternoon, she let her mind wander over the last twelve months, trying, once again, to pinpoint the underlying cause.

~

The previous year

The months after Christmas — even one understated — when the excitement of the season waned, were difficult, for Charlotte more so than the children. She began, gradually, to attend one or two events, wanting life to continue as normally as possible. The staff at the embassy were incredibly supportive, offering any assistance she might need in relation to the Sherbrooke assets in England, or her home in Paris. Charlotte appreciated their guidance.

Oliver had no surviving family other than his wife and children. He was an only child, his parents were dead, and he had no siblings or, as far as Charlotte knew, other relatives. Noah, previously a viscount in his own right — a title of which he had no awareness, had suddenly become the new Earl of Sherbrooke — another role he was far too young to undertake. Fortunately, Oliver's man of business, Mr Donaldson, along with several trusted stewards had been managing the family's holdings in their entirety — finances, land, and properties — since Oliver's secondment to Paris. This would not change. Further, Oliver had, with eerie foresight, amended his Will prior to their departure from

England. The addendum stipulated — in the event of him pre-deceasing his wife — Charlotte, as countess, would have full authority over Sherbrooke should Noah not be of age to assume his responsibilities.

Charlotte found the sheer volume of paperwork, and legal jargon therein, daunting. Mr Donaldson had returned to England shortly after Oliver's death to take charge of the Sherbrooke estates, meaning his replies to any questions she had, could take weeks to reach her. To Charlotte's surprise, Zacharie proved to be eminently knowledgeable about such things and, without making her feel ignorant, explained any terminology she found confusing.

Since then, and unobtrusively, Zacharie made himself available, periodically, by calling at *Maison de Sherbrooke* whenever he was in Paris. His visits never failed to brighten Charlotte's day, not to mention the children's — who instantly dragged him into whatever riotous game they were playing. Charlotte, wrestling to overcome her loss was grateful for his unflappable presence. Somehow, he always managed to make a molehill out of a mountain.

Charlotte, needing something to stop her from wallowing in misery and loneliness, and disinclined to waste her days doing nothing, undertook to volunteer at *Hôpital des Enfants Malades*. This was the hospital for sick children on the *rue de Sèvres*. Docteur Allard spoke highly of the innovative treatments employed there and accompanied Charlotte to meet the administrator, a M Dufort.

M Dufort, who never turned away genuine offers of assistance, was the only person who knew Charlotte's status. The Countess of Sherbrooke, concealing her identity by wearing unpretentious attire, became Madame Hastings, and no job was beneath her. She attended the hospital on the days her children were otherwise occupied and found it almost as rewarding as being a mother.

. . .

Augusta had departed at the beginning of March, wanting to be in London for the spring. Her coterie of friends had begun sending missives almost as soon as Christmas was over, demanding to know when she intended to return, having all manner of social events lined up. The children adjusted with apparent ease to their grandmama leaving — they had their own lives here in Paris, her presence was simply a bonus.

Noah's tantrums began shortly after. Initially, Charlotte was convinced it was because Augusta had left, yet another person in his life disappearing, but she was no longer certain this was the case.

〜

Present Day

Charlotte placed the sad-looking doll on the little table beside her chair and stood, shaking out her skirts. Walking over to the window, she wished for the millionth time that Oliver was here. He would know what to do, he always knew what to do. Charlotte loved her children, but Oliver was possessed of limitless patience where they were concerned, along with a knack for knowing how to get to the crux of the matter without fuss. *What do I do, Oliver?* Her silent plea going unanswered, as the sorrow she thought had subsided, pierced her with unexpected acuity. Staring out over the snowy garden, with unseeing eyes, Charlotte forced it aside and concentrated on how to reach Noah.

. . .

A rap at the door disturbed her introspection, and she turned to see Masson entering the room.

"My lady, Monsieur Romain is here and asks whether you are receiving."

Charlotte was aware of a slight revival of her spirits. Zacharie might understand Noah, he was male and had been a child, perhaps she would ask his advice.

"Thank you, Masson. Show him up but, should anyone else call, please let them know I am otherwise engaged this afternoon." She smiled at the butler who had been a pillar of strength this past year. Masson nodded and withdrew, returning moments later with Zacharie, whose hair was liberally sprinkled with snow.

Charlotte asked for coffee to be served, along with a brandy for Monsieur Romain.

"You should have seen me before Masson took my coat," Zacharie grinned when he spotted Charlotte's amused expression. "I resembled a snowman." Referring to the squat figures, children loved to build during the wintry weather. He walked across the room and bowed over her hand. "Good afternoon, my lady. I trust you are well."

Charlotte was startled by a curious frisson which snaked up her arm at Zacharie's touch. Covering her surprise, Charlotte ignored the sensation, thanked him, affirmed she was quite well, and invited him to sit.

"How does your business fare?" she enquired, at the same time as Masson came in bearing a tray on which stood two steaming coffees, a plate of sweet pastries, and a large brandy.

"Busy as ever," Zacharie replied, as he sipped the aromatic brew, relishing the taste. "Ahhh, that is good coffee."

They talked about this and that, circling around to the recently formed Trentams~Romain Shipping Company. Negotiations were finalised almost eight months previously, the two companies undergoing a seamless transition, and business was booming. While Charlotte listened to Zacharie's enthusiastic chatter, for the first time in several years, she felt the pull of

England. To be near her family, was suddenly appealing. Even if a couple of days' coach travel separated them, they were still easily reached. Here in Paris, England seemed as distant as the stars.

Maybe it was the problem with Noah which prompted her spasm of homesickness. Trying to get to the bottom of what was wrong might be easier in the bosom of her family.

Zacharie watched a multitude of expressions flit across Charlotte's face, perplexed as to the reason. "I beg your pardon, my lady, but you seem a trifle… discomposed. Is there anything I can do to mitigate your distress?"

"Oh, Zacharie, I am so sorry, 'Tis naught need worry you…" she trailed off, then heaved a sigh which seemed to come from her slippers. He *had* asked, and she *had* considered discussing her concerns with him. "No, that is not quite true…" she gave him a brief synopsis of Noah's behaviour. "It is so out of character. He was always such a happy-go-lucky child, floating through life without a care. This is as it should be, he is only eight, the concerns of the world ought not to bother him for at least another decade. Oliver would have known what to do, but I confess I am struggling. When Masson informed me of your presence, I felt a lifting of my heart, that perhaps your perspective might help."

Zacharie was possessed with the most extraordinary urge to enfold Charlotte in his arms and kiss her fears away. Shocked at his body's reaction, he inhaled a slow steadying breath. *Not the time, Zacharie,* he instructed himself, *honestly, man.*

CHAPTER 7

"My lady… Charlotte… he amended at her arched brow. He grinned self-consciously, "my apologies, 'tis discourteous being so informal.

"It is over a year since first I begged you to use my given name. From the day you escorted my family here from England, you have been as much a rock as Masson, maybe even more so. You refuse to answer me if I address you as Monsieur Romain," Charlotte tapped her finger against her chin, contemplatively, "I do believe 'tis only fair I return the favour. Henceforth, if you insist on calling me, my lady, or Lady Sherbrooke, I shall have no alternative but to pretend you are not here." Her tone was imperious, but her eyes twinkled with mischief.

Zacharie capitulated. "I will do my best. 'Tis not easy when I bear the utmost respect for you and your status. Neither do I wish anyone to think I am overstepping my position."

"Overstep…" Charlotte gaped at him and narrowed her eyes. "Zacharie Romain do not ever think that. Overstepping your position, goodness me, what nonsense. You are a trusted friend, a rare gift in this day and age. Now, about Noah…" she paused, her smoky gaze pinning Zacharie. "… do you have any suggestions?"

"I need you tell me in more detail when this started. Do there seem to be specific triggers, or are his bouts of temper random?"

Charlotte mulled this over. "Perhaps, it is easier for me just to tell you everything, and let you extract what's pertinent. There may be something I overlooked because I was too busy trying to prevent a repeat of his behaviour. I realise both Noah and Millie miss Oliver, that is inevitable, and I have tried to keep him alive in their minds. I talk about him frequently, recalling the things he liked to do, what made him laugh, and so on. Perhaps that has been my mistake. Mayhap they need to forget, maybe they find my reminders too painful." Charlotte opened her palms in entreaty, the gesture more eloquent than words.

"I agree, to tell me everything sounds the best approach. I am sure, between us we can get to the bottom of Noah's frustrations." Zacharie listened carefully while Charlotte unburdened her heart.

Two days had passed, and Charlotte remained in the dark regarding what transpired after Zacharie spoke to Noah. The latter was tracked down in the nursery where he and Millie, supervised by Elsa, their English nanny, were learning to play scales on an old piano. To be fair it sounded more like a herd of deer were stomping over the aged ivories — neither child proving to have a musical ear, and both balked at having to practise. Whatever Zacharie said seemed to have an effect, because her son was his normal, sunny self at dinner. The only reference Charlotte made to Zacharie's visit was to imply it had been solely to see Noah, whose face lit up at her seemingly casual remark.

Charlotte, however, noted his reaction and filed it away, hoping this was a turning point.

Sadly, it was not the case. Noah came home from school the following afternoon, in high dudgeon, and snarled at anyone who dared speak to him. Charlotte, who was already tired from an arduous day at the hospital, and with a headache nagging behind her eyes, refused to pander to his temper. Noah was dispatched to bed with a bowl of gruel… a dish he particularly detested.

Unbeknownst to Charlotte — in fact, unbeknownst to everyone, except perhaps one — Noah harboured a secret. Whenever he felt overwhelmed by the responsibilities, he believed lay on his shoulders, the child fled to a place no one would guess he even knew how to find, let alone choose to visit. A place of quiet reflection where he could sit undisturbed and unburden himself.

Noah only went when he was supposed to be at school, more often than not, precipitated by a thoughtless remark from one of his class mates. Politely, he would excuse himself, informing his tutor he was required at home. He was the Earl of Sherbrooke, he could do as he pleased, and it was the only time he flaunted his title. No one thought to challenge him. Without actually saying so, Noah implied he had received a summons and a carriage had been sent to collect him — thus his occasional absences were never mentioned to Charlotte.

He had visited this place often with Mama and knew the way with his eyes closed. On the days Noah floundered, it was as though an invisible hand reached out to clasp his, then led him, unerringly, to his destination. Once his equilibrium was restored, that same hand ushered him safely home. Mama would panic if she knew, and Noah had no intention of adding to her anxieties — his job was to prevent that at all costs. He never spoke of it, not even to his friends, who would have been astounded and impressed at his audacity.

If Noah ran, it did not take him long to get there, for he had discovered several short-cuts. He never went in inclement weather for fear his wet clothes would cause questions, neither did he go frequently — once a month seemed to suffice. Noah found solace in the tranquil setting, and those who surrounded him were guaranteed never to disclose his confidence.

When Charlotte awoke the next morning, her headache had worsened, and her throat was sore when she swallowed; her chest felt tight and she was overly warm. Measuring out a dose of one of Billie's remedies, Charlotte drank it down, screwing up her face at the taste, and praying it would do the trick. She did not have time to be unwell.

With Millie in tow, Charlotte walked Noah — who, mercifully, was in a better mood — to school. Mother and daughter returned home via one of the parks, where Millie ran about in the snow like a mad thing, making Charlotte laugh at her antics. It was a bitterly cold yet beautiful day; the sky was blue, and the sun was shining. Millie took this opportunity to sing very loudly, her voice echoing in the icy stillness, her warm breath expelled in little white puffs. Millie's behaviour might be viewed, by the stuffier members of Society, as unseemly but, to Charlotte, she was just a little girl letting off some steam after being cooped up in the house. There was no one about, and she wasn't causing any harm.

An hour later, they trudged up the steps into the domestic entrance of *Maison de Sherbrooke*, shedding coats, scarves, and boots, then slipping their feet into comfortable slippers warmed by the fire.

Millie went off to the nursery with Elsa for hot chocolate and a freshly baked biscuit or two. Charlotte, after advising Masson she would not be attending the hospital that day, went to the library, where she curled up on the chaise, in front of the roaring fire, and promptly fell asleep.

This was where Zacharie found her when he called mid-afternoon. She had not moved save it be necessary. Masson had brought a large blanket downstairs, asking Berthe — Charlotte's personal maid — to tuck it around her mistress. By luncheon,

Masson was anxious enough to suggest he send for Docteur Allard, but Charlotte waved aside his concerns saying she was probably just tired. When Zacharie arrived, Masson, greeting their guest, voiced his disquiet.

"I fear for Lady Sherbrooke's health. Last afternoon she complained of a headache, and today she seems feverish. She declined to have the doctor summoned and has been asleep for much of the day. After..." Masson pressed his lips together. It was not his place to remind Zacharie of what happened the last time someone was struck down by a fever in this house.

Zacharie patted the butler's shoulder, reassuringly. "Do not assume the worst, my friend. If I deem a physician is needed, I will bear the responsibility of sending for him." He could almost see Masson relax. Smiling, Zacharie handed the older man his coat, straightened his cravat and strode upstairs to the library.

Upon entering the room, Zacharie could see Charlotte was unwell. She was asleep, huddled under the blanket; her pallor only alleviated by the purplish shadows under her eyes. It was highly irregular — his being in the same room while she slept — but his relationship with the Sherbrookes had become more family than friend. Unwilling to rouse her, he took the chair adjacent to the chaise and studied her features. A veteran sailor who continued to captain his ships, Zacharie was familiar with the pathways of most of the deadly fevers. He was thankful to note, Charlotte did not seem to be exhibiting any of the typical symptoms and he deduced she had fallen prey to nothing more sinister than a nasty cold.

Aware he was taking liberties, Zacharie relished being able to observe Charlotte without constraint. Even in so miserable a state she was breathtakingly beautiful. Her lustrous black hair was unravelling from the neat bun Berthe had fashioned it into earlier that day, and her face, paler than usual, was like fine porcelain. Zacharie was torn between wanting her to wake up so he could lose himself in her grey gaze and prolonging this unforeseen opportunity.

Barely twenty minutes later, Charlotte awoke, spluttering apologies when she saw Zacharie sitting so close.

"Goodness, how appallingly rude of me. Zacharie, why did you, or Masson, not wake me? I am not so pathetic I cannot receive my friends."

Zacharie waved aside her apology. "Fret not, Charlotte. Masson is worried, and I assured him I was quite capable of ensuring you were not succumbing to an ailment which required the attendance of the physician. I ought to be the one apologising for seizing the chance to sit with you, undisturbed." He cursed his mouth for running ahead of his brain, but it was too late. His comment hung in the air between them and, in truth, he was not entirely sure he wanted to retract it. Zacharie had long ago acknowledged his feelings, when it came to Charlotte, were far more than simple concern for a young widow and her children.

CHAPTER 8

Charlotte felt her jaw drop, and twisted on the chaise until she faced him, her expression one of wide-eyed amazement. "*Pardon* me, might I beg you to repeat that?" she asked, her voice husky — and not just because of her cold.

Zacharie did so, adding, "I do not wish to ruin the friendship which has grown between us, neither do I want to place you in an awkward position, but I confess, friendship is only a small part of what I feel for you." Admitting what he had kept hidden for so long, sent a flood of unaccustomed heat across his face.

"Zacharie…" Charlotte gawked at the tall, ruggedly handsome man sitting alongside her, at the same time as her brain finally caught up with her heart. Those curious frissons which flickered through her whenever Zacharie was near; her elation when he called, even if it be just an hour, and the inexplicable melancholy after he departed, all suddenly made sense. Prior to this moment, she had been too caught up in loss, grief, and striving to keep life on an even keel, to identify them. No, no, no… how could she be falling in love with someone else? Oliver was her one and only.

She had two children. Neither of which quelled the wicked thrill which shot through her.

Zacharie spoke before she had time to form a lucid sentence. "I ought to say I am sorry, to withdraw my heedless remark, but I cannot. The day I met you, despite the sorrowful circumstances, you touched a part of me I thought long dead. Over the past year, without even trying, you have opened my eyes and my heart to a love I never expected to feel again. I know how deeply you love Oliver, and I have no desire to replace him in your heart, but I believe... I hope, you are not unmoved by me. Charlotte, I will humbly accept whatever crumbs you are prepared to scatter, even if that means continuing as we are, no more than friends."

Charlotte did not think she could be more astonished had Oliver's ghost manifest in front of her. Three things circled her poor, aching head. The most important being that Zacharie loved her... he *loved* her... *was she hearing things?* She ought to feel shocked and, to a certain extent she did, but the overriding emotion was one of joy, which in itself was significant. A warmth suffused her and, oddly, a weight she had no idea she carried, lifted. The second thing was that he referred to her love for Oliver as current, that he believed she continued to love her husband despite his death. Again, not altogether an erroneous assumption. Charlotte *did* still love Oliver, she would always love him, but he was part of her past. She missed him, and would never forget what they shared, but he was gone. To cling to something which could no longer be reciprocated, was unhealthy.

She could hear Oliver on the subject.

Tsk, Charlotte, my darling, do not spend the rest of your life living on a memory. Life is a gift; one which should be savoured, not taken for granted or wasted. Be brave, grasp every opportunity, sing, dance, laugh, and — yes, love. Never think you are being disrespectful to me by falling in love again.

Your happiness was my sole aim and I cannot bear to think you might miss out on discovering such happiness anew, because of some misguided sense of loyalty. Charlotte, you were my whole world, but I am gone. Open your heart — you were always the one to say 'let's try' — do you really want to spend the rest of your days wondering what if?

Embrace life, take a gamble — you never know where it might lead.

She smiled in reminiscence. It was true, she never balked at hurdles, she sought a way around or through them, but this was a gargantuan hurdle. Was the sentiment she bore for Zacharie, love, or a sense of gratitude for his solicitude?

She forced her recalcitrant mind back to the matter at hand, and the third thing Zacharie said… that she had 'opened his eyes and his heart to a love he never thought to feel again'.

"Zacharie…" once again, her mouth refused to follow instructions.

Zacharie, envisaging a rebuff interjected, "My lady, you are unwell, and this is not the time for personal discussions. Mayhap when you are less indisposed, we might revisit this conversation."

His formal address galvanised Charlotte.

"**No**! We will visit this conversation right this minute." She demanded hotly, finally getting her brain to work. "Firstly, Zacharie, I am honoured and humbled to be the one who elicits in you such emotions. Secondly, although I will always love Oliver," she noticed Zacharie flinch, and hastened to reassure, "he is dead. No amount of prayers or pleas will bring him back, and he would be devastated if he thought I had put my life on hold because he is no longer by my side. I admit, I did not imagine ever experiencing a similar depth of devotion for another but," Charlotte stretched out her hand, resting it on Zacharie's knee, "this attraction developing between us is undeniable and something, I believe, worth exploring."

Charlotte's fiery response surprised Zacharie, but her next words sent his stomach plummeting. As anticipated, she was going to inform him, graciously, she did not reciprocate his feelings. What was he thinking anyway? Her love for Oliver had evidently been the forever kind, he was a fool to think she could move on, so soon after his death. Then she shocked him. She *did* care... he met her gaze, and her ash-grey eyes held him captive.

"Ch-Charlotte..." his tongue seemed to have swollen, he could not make his mouth do his bidding. He searched her face, watching the smile curve those perfect lips. God, he wanted to kiss her... "...s-sorry, w-words... sure... not just p-pity..." he clamped his own lips closed. *Merde, he sounded like a babbling idiot.*

"Zacharie..." he heard a hint of censure in her tone, "...pity? For shame. What need have you of my pity? I concede, had you never initiated this discourse, it is likely my life would have continued as it has for the past year. Although..." she paused, then continued pensively, "perhaps not. Fate, rather curiously, saw fit to place you in my path. Thus, our meeting and subsequent affection was undoubtedly predestined. Your beautiful words today merely precipitated the inevitable."

While she spoke, Charlotte's voice had weakened to a croak and she pressed her hand to her forehead. "Forgive me, Zacharie. I want to talk with you, I want to know what you meant when you said a love you never thought to feel again, but my head is pounding, and my throat is so sore." She paused and, frustrated with herself for sounding so feeble, added in a piteous whisper, "I do not want you to leave me."

"My darling, may I call you my darling?" Zacharie asked. He rose from his chair and, after pulling the bell-rope, moved to sit beside Charlotte on the chaise. She nodded, shyly. "My darling, I think bed is the best place for you. Permit me to carry you to your room. With Berthe's help we shall get you tucked in and, perhaps after you sip another dose of Bill… Lady Winchester's famous tincture, you will rest undisturbed."

"The children…" Charlotte felt she ought to protest, to say she could manage, but she felt thoroughly miserable, and the thought of bed was irresistible.

"Berthe and I will look after them. Do not fret, my love." The door of the library opened to admit Masson. "Ah, Masson, I am taking Lady Sherbrooke to her bedchamber, might you ask Berthe to come and assist?"

Masson, in quick understanding hurried to find Berthe, then went to the kitchen where he asked cook to brew up her cure-all hot, sweet drink, which contained a generous dollop of honey and a dash of brandy. Once it was prepared, Masson added a measure of the rather foul-tasting concoction Lady Winchester assured them was just the thing for a nasty cold.

In the meantime, Zacharie carried Charlotte upstairs to her bedchamber, where he encountered Berthe. Stepping outside, he fidgeted restlessly, unsure whether he ought to return to the library and await the children, behave as Society would demand and leave, or do as Charlotte requested and stay with her. Masson appeared, bearing the hot drink, and ushered Zacharie back into the room.

"I doubt my Lady will rest until she is satisfied herself you are still here." Masson smiled. Confirmed seconds later, when Charlotte's eyes flitted across the three people in her room, seeking Zacharie's. She smiled wanly and reached out her hand. He went to her bedside and without thinking, laced their fingers together.

"Sit with me," she beseeched, inclining her head towards the chair next to the bed. Zacharie hesitated. Charlotte frowned and tugged on his hand. "Please."

Sending a helpless glance over his shoulder at the butler and the maid, Zacharie sank onto the seat. Charlotte refused to relinquish her grip, accepting the cup containing the hot drink with her other hand.

Masson left after giving Berthe a quiet instruction. The maid

nodded and went to sit in a chair by the fire. This gave the couple
a little privacy, but propriety was not abandoned. Despite Lady
Sherbrooke being a widow, and thus accorded a modicum of
independence compared with the majority of her peers, Masson
had no mind for her to become the target of spiteful gossip.

Peace enveloped the room; the only sound was the crackling
of wood in the hearth. When Charlotte finished her drink,
Zacharie took the cup, and placed it on the table next to her bed.
Shuffling against the pillows, Charlotte's gaze landed on their
conjoined hands. She tried to corral her muddled thoughts, still
dumbfounded she had failed to notice the signs which, in retro-
spect, were obvious. At some point, Zacharie's subtle gallantry,
quiet kindness, and tender consideration had melted her heart.

"Thank you," she rasped, squeezing his fingers.

Greatly daring, Zachary leaned over and brushed his lips to
her hot forehead. "Sleep, my love."

"Will you stay?" She stared into his eyes, hers starting to glaze
over.

"I will stay until you no longer have need of me."

Charlotte smiled, drowsily, her eyelids drooping. "So, forever
then," she murmured, sliding down the pillows.

"If that is your desire, then so be it." Zacharie's formal tones
were belied by his smile — wide as the Seine, and the joy which lit
his face.

"That is my desire," her words slurring as slumber and the
infusion, began to weave their spell.

"I love you, Charlotte."

"I lov…" and she was asleep.

Zacharie waited until he was certain his movements would not
disturb Charlotte, then gently disengaged their hands, and walked
over to the window. Staring across the garden, the snowy scene
glimmering in shades of gold and red under the dying rays of the
sun, he let his thoughts roam. In the space of an afternoon, his

world had spun out of all recognition. Charlotte loved him. It was astonishing how her declaration reanimated his soul. He felt a curious sense of promise, of anticipation, threaded through with a happiness he thought never to find again.

Yes, he still had to tell her about Nathalie, but he did not foresee Charlotte's reaction to be anything other than empathetic. They had both suffered a bereavement, but that made the telling easier. Each understood how loss affected a person; to be brought to your knees — figuratively and literally — by the nagging fear you no longer knew how to breathe, to live. Zacharie was not a foolish young bachelor, given to romantic tarradiddle — he was a sea-hardened sailor, a practical and astute businessman, but there was something about Charlotte which had turned him into a love-sick calf. She had revived him, infused life back into his jaded heart, kindling a spark which had been lying dormant in readiness for her to ignite.

He turned away from the wintry scene and it seemed, with so negligible a gesture, his past was consigned to memory. He stared at Charlotte, fast asleep under layers of luxurious covers, her raven hair splayed across the white pillows. He studied her pale face, her dark lashes a sooty smudge above reddened cheeks. He smiled, even in the throes of fever she enchanted him; she was his love, his hopes, his dreams… his future.

During the subsequent week, Zacharie endeared himself to Charlotte's household, not only through the care he lavished on Charlotte, but also because of the amount of time he spent with the children.

Both Noah and Millie were, predictably, upset when Zacharie explained about their mother's illness. Noah, especially so.

"She's going to die just like Papa," was the boy's immediate and implacable response when Zacharie explained that Charlotte was confined to bed.

"No, lad, your Mama has a cold. She feels off colour and needs to sleep. Trust me when I say she will be up and about before you know it." Zacharie presumed this would be enough to reassure the child. Not so. Noah worked himself into a fine tantrum, stomping up and down the drawing room waving his hands about, refusing to listen to reason.

"You are a liar! Papa died, now Mama will die, they all die. She is probably already dead, and you are keeping it a secret!" Noah roared. His face was puce with temper, and the irrational outburst prompted Millie to burst into tears.

"M-mama is d-dead?" she stammered and flung herself at Zacharie. Although Zacharie had spent time with both the Sherbrooke children, Millie rarely conversed with him. The little girl was comfortable in his presence, but until this moment had been content to let Noah monopolise the tall man's attention. When together, Noah and Zacharie talked of ships and the sea, the latter spinning tales of pirates and naval battles. Millie listened to one or two, then got bored — she preferred the *conte des fées*, much more exciting. When she heard Noah shouting about Mama being dead, she remembered her Papa, cold and still in the bed, and panic overrode her usual reserve. Millie clung to Zacharie, sobbing as though her little heart would break.

Zacharie arched an exasperated brow at Noah — who had the grace to look sheepish but continued to grumble under his breath — then sat on the nearest chair and rocked the little girl until her sobs lessened into pitiful hiccups. "Millie, Millie, *ma choupette,* do not weep. Your Mama is not dead. She is upstairs fast asleep. If you give me your word you will not wake her, I shall take you to see her."

Millie lifted her head, and pinned Zacharie with a rather watery, dark grey gaze. "I promise."

Zacharie stood her on the floor. "Then come with me. Noah,

please join us." His tone, although gentle, brooked no argument. The three trooped upstairs to Charlotte's bedchamber. At the door Zacharie felt a small hand slip into each of his. He hid a smile and asked them to be quiet as mice. They crept over to the bed where their mother lay, deep in slumber. Despite the tell-tale signs that Charlotte was feverish, Zacharie surmised her breathing sounded less laboured. A bronchitis kettle hung over the fire, the steam — infused with what smelt like menthol — permeated the room, doubtless easing Charlotte's symptoms.

"There, you see Mama is just asleep. Noah, do you believe me now?" Speaking in undertones, Zacharie looked down at Noah who shuffled awkwardly then nodded. "*Bien.* That is settled, now we must leave your Mama in peace." When the door closed behind them, he added, "I wonder whether cook has anything tasty in the kitchen?"

"Ohhhhh…" Millie turned a bright gaze on him while Noah did a little jig.

"Lead the way." said Zacharie, allowing himself to be dragged to the domestic quarters where cook was prevailed upon to provide a slice of luscious cake.

That was three days ago and, since then, the two children had behaved in a manner of which their mother would be proud.

Charlotte, given strict instructions to stay in bed, capitulated and was feeling much more human again. Her voice was still a bit croaky, but her throat was no longer sore, and the headache had finally dissipated. The snatches of time she was wakeful she spent either pondering Noah's tantrums or relishing Zacharie's attentiveness. Now she was on the mend, Charlotte really wanted to know what kissing Zacharie would be like… he had been the soul of discretion these past few days, but it was driving her to distraction. His touch was enough to increase her heart rate and the occasional brush of his lips to her forehead sent heat spiralling from her core. Damn him for being such a gentleman… she was determined to tap into his piratical side… he had been a sailor… he *must* have one.

CHAPTER 10

One Friday afternoon, in the middle of a snowstorm at the beginning of February, Noah's baffling outbursts came to a head. Only Zacharie's quick thinking, averted another tragedy.

Charlotte, long restored to full health, was on tenterhooks. That morning she received a missive from Zacharie — whose business commitments recalled him to London nigh on three weeks previously — apprising her of his return to Paris and he hoped to call on her that afternoon. Since her recovery, the most intimate they had been was to walk arm in arm to the local park with the children — twice, and a single kiss to the back of her hand. To Charlotte's frustration, with one thing and another, they had not been alone *at all*. They *had* written to one another while apart, letters describing their busy days, and quiet evenings — unexpectedly lonely. Endearments, however toe-curling, flowing onto the creamy paper in abundance were not nearly enough to assuage a longing yet to be fulfilled

For almost the whole period of Zacharie's absence, the weather in Paris had been exceptional. A cloudless blue sky kept the temperatures well below freezing, but this along with the bright sunshine were a welcome respite from days of gloomy grey. Advised by Docteur Allard to delay resuming her visits to the hospital for another week or so, Charlotte took advantage of the break in the weather. With Masson's assistance, she planned outings to places around and beyond Paris which might be of interest to youngsters... no easy feat. Then, every afternoon, when Noah had finished his lessons, she hustled her children into the carriage, and they went on an adventure.

This proved a great success and, if some of the places they explored, coincidentally, expanded their knowledge of the history of this beautiful city, neither child was aware. First on Charlotte's list, *le jardin des Tuileries*. A favourite park, it was somewhere the family had visited regularly when Oliver was alive, especially during the summer months, and an obvious choice for somewhere to let children expend their seemingly tireless energies. The lush green swathes of lawn and verdant hues of myriad trees had given way to a glistening winter wonderland in countless shades of white. Against the backdrop of an azure sky it was breathtaking.

"Oh, Mama, 'tis magical," was Millie's considered opinion, her eyes and mouth forming matching 'O's when their carriage rolled through the gates. A sentiment with which her doting mother was inclined to agree. With absolutely no mind to be decorous, Noah and Mille charged about in the snow, tossing handfuls in the air, shrieking with laughter when one of them tumbled into a drift. There were few others abroad, and Charlotte let her children have their fun. To see them so cheerful was far more important than worrying about whether their madcap capers upset anyone. The lake was frozen, and they all rocked with mirth at the poor waterfowl attempting to land on, and forage through, the ice. This idyllic entertainment set the bar for the subsequent sojourns. To be declared better than *le jardin des Tuileries* was praise indeed.

Another afternoon was taken up visiting the *Arc de Triomphe* at the western end of the *Champs Élysée*. The imposing arch, inspired — so Charlotte was reliably informed — by the Arch of Titus in Rome, was conceived by Napoleon to honour those who died in the French Revolutionary and Napoleonic wars. Begun in 1806, work had been halted for over a decade, and, alas, there did not seem to be any hurry to recommence. Architecture on a grand scale, fascinated Noah. He could spend hours studying the façades of historical structures and landmarks — like the *Musée du Louvre*, or the stunning buildings in the *Place des Vosges*. Charlotte deliberately included expeditions to such places, purely for Noah's benefit. His cheerful smile and excited chatter had been sorely lacking of late.

Both Noah and Millie were in awe of the Church of *Ste-Geneviève* — Geneviève being the patron saint of Paris — or as some referred to it *Le Panthéon*. Once inside, Charlotte, who had done her homework, began to explain the different architectural styles, only to have Noah intervene and elaborate on her, admittedly limited, knowledge. His understanding of the techniques astounded Charlotte, who found herself asking *him* about the coffers, and the columns, and the cleverly constructed ceiling rather than the other way around. Millie, on the other hand, was quite happy standing under the soaring central dome and singing — elated to hear her sweet treble reverberate around the lofty interior, then drift back to her in unearthly echoes.

Despite the length of time they had lived in Paris, this was the first time any of them had been inside this incredible edifice, and all were suitably impressed. Charlotte had also hoped to show her children the *Notre Dame de Paris* but was advised against this owing the cathedral's woeful state of disrepair. A walk around the exterior, trying to spot the grotesques had to suffice.

They enjoyed a boat ride on the Seine, took excursions beyond the city, ate picnics — usually snugly wrapped up in the carriage — and discovered several more parks. Towards the end of the second week, Charlotte took Noah to *les Catacombs des Paris*. The ossuary had become a macabre attraction in recent years, and although Charlotte had no burning desire to see it, she suspected her son would relish the opportunity to wander the underground caverns.

This was one occasion when Charlotte decided Millie ought to stay at home; she was too young for what Charlotte envisioned would be nightmare-provoking sights. Millie was further persuaded when cook, primed by Charlotte, asked the little girl to help bake some treats. Knowing her daughter would end up with more ingredients on her than in anything she made, Charlotte thanked her long-suffering cook, and left them to an afternoon of hilarity.

Fortuitously, Masson was related to one of the overseers and, by dint of dropping their titles, obtained permission for the diminutive earl, and Lady Sherbrooke to be granted a personal tour. Charlotte, questioning her sanity, her skin crawling with scarcely suppressed horror, had to clamp her lips together throughout much of the visit. In the eerie glow from lamps positioned at infrequent intervals along the passageways and the one carried by their guide, they passed walls of bones and skulls, displays of skeletal deformities, funerary artefacts, and huge stone tablets bearing sinister inscriptions. Noah, not in the slightest fazed was fascinated by the whole experience and peppered their guide with a multitude of questions regarding the facts and figures of the catacombs.

Charlotte was heartily glad when they climbed back into the half-light of the waning afternoon. Sucking in the chill fresh air, she declared, to Noah's glee — never again. Upon their return to *Maison de Sherbrooke*, they were presented with an array of dubiously shaped tartlets, painstakingly made by a righteously pleased and slightly smudged, Millie. A memorable afternoon was had by all.

~

At this time of the year, days of uninterrupted sunshine were the exception not the rule. Before long, the weather closed in again, effectively curbing any further adventures for the time being, and confining everyone to the house. Blizzards and howling winds rendered any outside activities, pointless.

When she received Zacharie's letter, Charlotte was astonished he had risked the Channel crossing in such inclement conditions. Even though she knew he took every precaution with his crews and vessels, and would never intentionally place either in jeopardy, Charlotte was glad she was unaware he had been at sea during the storms.

Now he was hours, nay minutes, away from being in the same house, and Charlotte was unnerved by the gamut of sensations rippling through her. She had not behaved like this since the first time Oliver came to call. She had changed her gown... three times, had Berthe fix her hair, then do it again, eventually opting for a neat plait twisted into a bun, and still could not chose a pair of slippers. Honestly, she was hopeless.

In the far reaches of her consciousness, she heard Oliver chuckle...

Charlotte, my darling, Zacharie loves you. He declared his love when you were in the midst of a fever, all mussed and rumpled. An unsuitable, in your mind, pair of shoes is unlikely to sway his devotion.

"Typical," she grumbled under her breath, "no sense of occasion." Hearing Oliver's laughter fade when she spotted a pair of charcoal, kid-leather slippers, the perfect complement to the dark-teal hue of her dress. Standing, she stroked nerveless fingers over her silk skirts, removing invisible wrinkles and, with a last glance in the mirror, went along to the library. Hopefully, she could distract herself by reading one of the many books adorning the shelves.

CHAPTER 11

At precisely two o'clock, Masson heard a loud rapping. Opening the front door, he smiled at who was standing on the step.

"Ahhh… Monsieur Romain, please come in. Her ladyship is expecting you." He took the Frenchman's coat and led him upstairs. Knocking on the door of the library, he entered, and announced their guest.

Charlotte, a bundle of nerves, remained in her chair, totally unable to make her legs hold her. "M Rom… Zacharie," she greeted him with a guarded smile. "I hope your voyage was not too… errr… choppy. "

Zacharie bowed. "*Bonjour,* my lady. It was a little squally, but not too bad, thank you for asking." His tone softened. "'Tis glad I am to see you." He heard the quiet click of the door closing and took one step. Pausing, he scanned her face, perceiving a wariness, a shyness in the boundless grey depths of her eyes. "I missed you."

"I m-missed you m-more," Charlotte stammered, hectic colour flooding her cheeks. She stood, then sat down again, shaking her head. "S-sorry… I… m-maybe… do you… oh dear…" she petered out, coherence abandoning her just when she needed a sensible tongue in her head.

In four strides, Zacharie was at her side. He took her hand and drew her up from the chair. She angled her head to study his face — his devastatingly, handsome face. His dark brown hair neatly caught in a queue — her fingers itched to undo it — his mesmerising green eyes bore into her, holding her spell-bound.

"Zacharie…" his name on her lips a petition.

"Yes, my lady,"

"Don't be such a gentleman…"

Zacharie's mouth curved in a wicked grin, and requiring no second bidding, moulded her against his burly frame, his hand splayed over her back anchoring her to him.

"I love you," he kissed her forehead.

"I missed you," he kissed her nose.

"I love you," he traced a line of featherlight kisses along her jawline to the soft skin behind her ear.

Clinging to him, her senses awry, Charlotte heard a moan… *goodness but she was a hussy.* "Z-Zacharie…" she whimpered, her head falling back, and he blazed a trail down her throat to her décolletage. "Oh God, Zacharie… please…" knowing what she wanted, but unable to articulate it. All she could manage was, "…I love you."

He groaned, then crushed his mouth to hers.

Charlotte responded, opening to him, shuddering when his tongue met hers, tasting the sweetness. Fire coiled through her, licking along her veins, her body becoming molten. His hands roamed over her body and she wanted to feel them on her skin, not just on the silk of her dress… although the rustle of the material *was* rather sensuous. Their kiss went on and on, ardour rising.

Uncaring how it looked, Charlotte fiddled with Zacharie's cravat — noticing, absently, it was the one she gave him the previous Christmas — removing and flinging it somewhere behind her. Inquisitive fingers undid the buttons of his juniper-green waistcoat, pushing it off his shoulders — the satin landing on the rug with quiet swish. Like a woman possessed, she yanked his shirt out of his trousers, sighing audibly when her hands finally brushed against his flesh.

"Zacharie..." she whispered, seemingly unable to utter any word but his name. Stretching up, on tiptoe, she pressed a kiss to the v of exposed skin at the neckline of his shirt.

"Charlotte..." Zacharie, aware of how much he wanted the beauty in his arms, tried to control his visceral reaction to her ministrations. The urge to make love to her in front of a roaring fire, on this luxurious rug was almost overwhelming, but he knew the door was unlocked, the children, or any of her staff could bustle in without warning. When Charlotte and he became intimate, Zacharie wanted to take his time, to make it last, to spend hours and hours discovering every inch of her, then doing it all over again... and again... and again. He caught her wandering hands and brought them behind her, trapping her against him.

Drawing a ragged breath, he murmured. "Not here... well, yes here... but not yet. Charlotte, *mon amour, je t'aime, je t'adore*. I cannot imagine spending another moment without you. Please bestow on me the greatest honour and agree to marry me." Zacharie's mix of French and English was almost Charlotte's undoing. His Gallic accent sending quivers tumbling down her spine.

"Y-you w-want to *m-marry* me?" Her voice, despite rising in astonishment, thrummed with desire, the flames only he could stoke, slowly, but inexorably consuming her.

"*Mais oui, vraiment,*" he sounded surprised at her question. "You think I make a habit of kissing women, *mon trésor? Non,* you are the only woman I have kissed for longer than I care to recall."

His words reminded Charlotte of his curious comment the afternoon he admitted his love for her. She leaned back in his embrace and cupped his cheek, her heart thudding. "*Mon cœur,*" smiling when his eyes widened. "*Ah oui, je parle un peu français,*" then she reverted to English. "My darling, what did you mean when you said I opened your heart to a love you never thought to feel again?"

Zacharie flushed. He had just proposed marriage, now was not the time to be talking about a love long dead. "I do not think…"

Charlotte's finger came to rest on his lips. "Zacharie, there should be no secrets. You asked me to marry you, and I intend to say yes, but before I do, I need to know who shattered your heart. I realise this person, this lady, is no longer in your life, but she is part of who you are, who you were. Perhaps we ought to afford each other the trust of sharing our past." She cocked her head, holding his eyes, her gaze tender with compassion.

Charlotte's, 'I intend to say yes,' made Zacharie's heart soar, and he had to force himself to concentrate on the remainder of her point. She was right, despite the years since Nathalie's death, she was more a shade between them than Oliver. He planted a searing kiss on unsuspecting lips, leaving Charlotte gasping.

"You are correct, *ma chérie*, come let us sit, and I will tell you about Nathalie."

When they were comfortably settled on the chaise — Zacharie sitting almost formally, Charlotte curled up beside him, her head pillowed on his shoulder, her right hand entwined with his left — Zacharie started to speak. He told of a young sailor and the auburn-haired maiden who stole his heart. Nathalie and he grew up in the same small fishing village on the French coast, but when he was sent to England, Zacharie supposed never to see her again.

He was surprised therefore, when they met on a street in Dieppe, scant weeks after his return to France to take over his father's shipping business. Their youthful friendship quickly became something more, and within three months, they were married. Neither had family to approve their nuptials, and the war left people with the notion that life was fleeting, and not to waste a moment. Two years later Nathalie was dead. She fell victim to complications during childbirth, and neither the midwife nor the physician was able to save her or their daughter.

While he spoke, Zacharie became aware of a grief, he presumed long diminished, welling, and could not hold back his tears, cursing himself for such weakness. He tried to turn away, to mask his anguish. He should not be weeping for Nathalie in front of his new love, the love for whose hand he had just asked — how crass. He sensed rather than saw Charlotte shift position.

Shuffling until she was on her knees on the chaise, Charlotte slid one arm around his shoulders while her other hand cupped his face, her thumb resting on the corner of his mouth. She waited until he looked at her.

"*Mon amour* do not hide your sorrow from me. You, who have watched over me since first we met. You, who have seen me break down into helpless sobs because a flower reminded me of Oliver. You, who without fuss have lifted my burdens, and become the backbone of my family throughout our own grief. You, who ensured I talked about my life with Oliver, until my heartache eased. You, who showed no trepidation in declaring your love for me, not knowing whether it was reciprocated. My love, admitting to sadness is no frailty, 'tis courageous, and to suppress such a debilitating emotion means it can never be allayed. Trust me, I know."

Allowing Zacharie a moment to compose himself, Charlotte used her handkerchief to dab at the dampness under his eyes. Stretching, she kissed the tracks of his tears, then brushed her lips to his, the stubble ghosting along his craggy jaw, tickling her skin.

"Ask me again," she murmured into his ear, biting the soft lobe.

"*Mon amour*, will you marry me?"

"*Bien sûr*, nothing would give me greater happiness than to be your wife."

"*Dieu merci*, thank God," he smiled down at her and, before she could protest — not that there was any likelihood of her doing so — pulled her onto his knee. His right hand cradled the nape of her neck, his left arm wrapped round her waist, bringing her flush against him. "And now I must kiss you again, it is the only way to seal the proposal."

Which he did… most satisfactorily.

CHAPTER 12

So pre-occupied were they by their mounting passion, neither heard the muffled thunder of feet along the carpeted hall or were conscious of the door bursting open. Nothing until the clapping of hands and an excited voice broke through the haze.

"Zacharie, Zacharie, are you going to marry Mama?" Noah was hopping about less than a foot away, a broad grin on his face which was wreathed in jubilation.

Charlotte blushed and, with as much dignity as she could muster, stood and smoothed her skirts, patting her hair which was unravelling from its neat style. Before she could respond, Zacharie interposed.

"Yes, I have asked your mama to marry me and she has agreed. However, I should also like to beg your permission."

Noah gawked at the tall Frenchman. "Why do you want to ask me?" He canted his head, his dark eyes studying Zacharie, suspiciously.

Zacharie crouched on the floor until he was eye level with the boy. "Because you are the most important man in her life."

"I am?" His expression attesting to his surprise.

Charlotte could see this had not crossed his mind. She sat on the chaise and drew her son to her side. "Noah, you have always been, and always will be the most important man in my life. You are my son, my firstborn."

"B-but what of Papa, and Millie, and Zacharie. Are they not important?"

"Of course, but in different ways." Unwilling to get into a complex discussion about levels of importance and why, Charlotte concluded with… "You will understand when you are older."

Noah seemed to accept this, his mind shooting off on another tangent. "Does this mean when you marry Zacharie, he will be the earl?"

Charlotte smiled reassuringly, thinking to placate his worry. "No, my sweet, Zacharie will be my husband, but the title remains yours. You inherited that from your Papa, like a precious gift. No one can take it away; it belongs to you."

There was an odd hiss. Charlotte watched Noah clench his fists, his face flushing scarlet as his anger erupted.

"Do you mean to say, even after you marry Zacharie, I still have to be a bloody earl? I do not want it. I hate this stupid title, I hate Zacharie, and I hate you. You are all blackguards," he spat.

Charlotte was so confounded by Noah's invective, she barely registered his underlying complaint, and was struck dumb for several minutes during which Noah stomped around the room, roaring his fury. Gathering herself, Charlotte — determined not to let him ruin her lovely afternoon — sent Noah to his room.

"Perhaps after an hour alone you will come to your senses. I am mortified a son of mine would be so appallingly rude. I thought, I hoped we taught you better than that." Charlotte's stern voice and outraged expression leaving Noah in no doubt of her ire. In turn, he bellowed another tirade at his mother… at the world. Clearly, there would be no reasoning with him while he was in such a vile temper. Noah stalked out of the library, slamming the door with such force it rattled.

. . .

Charlotte was trembling with shock and distress. "I am sorry you are witness, nay, subject to that, Zacharie. I am at my wit's end. How is it possible for a child to be so cheerful one moment and so furious the next?"

Zacharie took Charlotte in his arms and kissed her gently. "I cannot tell, but I am sure we shall uncover the source of his wrath." His use of the word 'we' instead of 'you' resonated with Charlotte. That Zacharie already thought in terms of togetherness warmed her. "There was something…" he paused and replayed the scene in his head. "Noah was pleased, almost ecstatic when we told him we are to be wed, then…" he ruminated for several minutes. Snapping his fingers, he said with satisfaction. "I think I have it."

"Please, what is it?"

"I fear he is troubled at having to assume the mantle of earl."

Charlotte stared at him, stunned. "He's what?"

Zacharie repeated his suspicion and elaborated. "When you affirmed the title was his, that I could not take it from him, his whole countenance darkened, and his joy vanished."

"I cannot credit it, could the answer be *so* rudimentary? All this time a mere title was the thing which roused his anger, caused his upset? How did I not see this? What kind of a mother am I to miss something which, now you have suggested it, should have been blindingly obvious?" She closed her eyes, inky lashes sweeping over ivory skin.

"Charlotte Sherbrooke, you are a wonderful mother. Noah has had every opportunity to tell you, to explain what vexed him, and for whatever reason chose not to. That is not something you can blame yourself for. Now we know, or at least we think we know, let us hope we can get to the bottom of it." He kissed her nose, glad to see a half-smile curve her lips. "Come, no time like the present. This needs to be dealt with sooner rather than later. The longer Noah allows it to fester the more insurmountable it will seem."

"Thank you," she moved into him, looped her arms around his waist, and laid her head on his chest. The regular beat of his heart, soothing.

"What for?" He leaned back slightly so he could look down at her and raised a quizzical brow.

"Loving me."

"That works both ways, *ma chérie.*" He pressed his lips to her hair and, taking her hand, they headed upstairs to Noah's bedchamber.

The door was ajar, and Charlotte's knock was met with silence. "Noah, may we come in?" No reply, just dead air. Pushing open the door, Charlotte peered in. Not a sign of Noah. She walked right into the room, his bedclothes were in a tangled heap in the middle of the bed, toys and books were strewn across the floor. To all appearances it was as though a whirlwind had blown through.

"Charlotte…" Zacharie began, concern in his voice and etched on the angular planes of his face. Charlotte shook her head.

"Fret not, my love, there is nothing unusual here, save his absence. Noah seems to think this is an acceptable way to leave his bedchamber. No amount of chastising seems to have any effect."

Zacharie chuckled and felt an elbow to his ribs.

"Do not laugh. I want him to understand what a privilege it is to have staff who tidy up after him, after us. Papa always taught us to value those whom we employ, they work hard to keep us in comfort, they deserve our utmost respect."

Zacharie held up his hands. "You have no need to convince me. I have experienced both sides, and but for the grace of God…" he let that hang. "So where is Noah?"

"He has probably snuck down to the kitchens to bemoan his

punishment and beg a treat," Charlotte posited. "I daresay, Masson will know." Going over to the bell-rope by the door, she gave it a tug, then walked into the hallway and stood, her hands resting on the balustrade, staring into space, running over scenarios in her head. Within a minute the genial butler was walking towards them along the corridor. "Masson, have you perchance seen Noah this afternoon?"

"Not since his return from lessons, my lady."

"Strange," Charlotte tapped her foot. "He might be angry with me, but he has never disobeyed me. Masson, please have the staff look for my son, especially in the garden. She glanced across the hall to the window adjacent to the staircase as the butler hurried off to deliver her instructions. Snowflakes, whipped into a dizzying dance by the strengthening breeze, hurled themselves at the glass. Visibility was almost nil. Charlotte heaved a sigh. *Where was Noah?*

An hour later, every inch of *Maison de Sherbrooke* had been searched.

Of Noah there was no sign.

CHAPTER 13

S tanding in the middle of the spacious entrance hall, wringing her hands together, Charlotte was frantic. Where on earth could Noah be? They were stumped. The day was waning, it was almost dusk, and the snow continued to fall.

"Zacharie what do we do? Where do we look? What if he ran away? 'Tis nearly dark and he's only eight, I know he has been acting like a little devil of late, but he's my little devil and I love him, and he's only eight…" Charlotte's voice rose on a wail.

"Try not to fret, we will find him. Come, let us talk to Masson and Elsa, perhaps even Millie. She may be only five, but there is possibility she overheard something Noah said which might help."

Acknowledging the sense in this, Charlotte walked over to the wall and pulled the bell. Masson appeared. Charlotte asked him to find Elsa and Millie, and for them all to join her and Zacharie in the library. Masson hurried off and, moments later, the small group had gathered in the cosy room.

Zacharie took charge. "As you are aware, we have not found Noah. I must ask, can you think of anywhere, anywhere at all, he might go, if upset — even if it seems improbable."

Masson and Elsa shook their heads, unable to offer any further suggestions.

Millie said nothing, but her expression spoke volumes. To those watching, it was clear she was arguing with herself about something important. Zacharie sat on the floor and looked at Millie. In a gentle tone, he elaborated. "Perhaps Noah has a secret place. Somewhere only he goes to, the whereabouts of which he may have whispered to his sister, because he wanted to sound important, but then begged her not to tell anyone else." Millie stared at him wide-eyed, chewing on her bottom lip. "Do you know of such a place, *ma choupette?*"

The little girl fidgeted, lifting her gaze to her mother before swinging it back to Zacharie.

Charlotte sank onto the rug next to Zacharie and took Millie's hand. "Please tell us, sweetheart. It is very cold outside, and Noah might not find his way home in all this snow. 'Tis easy to take a wrong turn." She kept her voice calm, encouraging.

For a long — and for some, tortuous — moment, the room was silent, then…

"Noah *does* have a secret place he likes to visit. It has statues and pieces of stone with letters carved on them. He says he can talk to Papa when he is there. I wanted him to take me, I wanted to talk to Papa, but he said it was only for boys." Millie's face crumpled. "I don't want Noah to be lost." Her reedy voice cracked, and tears spilled down her cheeks. In spite of her fear for Noah, Charlotte knew Millie's need in that instant, was greater. Pulling the child into her arms, she hugged her daughter, closing her eyes and breathing in her childish scent. *Would this ever stop? Would Oliver's death forever haunt them? Was she being fair inflicting all this on Zacharie?*

She felt a hand stroke over hers and opened her eyes, straight into Zacharie's tender gaze.

"I love you, Charlotte, and you are all my family now. Your trials are mine. Your joys are mine. Moreover, I believe Oliver has given his approval." He smiled and squeezed the hand he had been stroking.

Charlotte frowned, puzzled. She opened her mouth to question his last remark, when Millie shrugged out of her arms and slid across her mother's knee to where Zacharie was still sitting on the floor.

"Papa, please find Noah," she beseeched.

With a huge effort, Zacharie managed to hide his astonishment. Charlotte simply gawked — there was no other word for it.

Millie hooked her little arms around his neck and planted a — more than likely sticky — kiss on his cheek. Then she patted his other cheek and smiled. "I know you can find him."

Zacharie opened his mouth to reply but nothing came out, the words stuck in his throat. The faith this small child had in him was humbling. He tried again, this time he managed a croak. "I promise." He assured and kissed the top of her head. "Now run along with Elsa. Masson, your Mama, and I, will fetch Noah."

Charlotte began to stammer an interruption. They still did not know where Noah was. Millie's comments made no sense. Zacharie caught her eye and shook his head. Charlotte swallowed and gave Millie another hug saying they would be home with her brother very soon.

Millie, sucking her thumb, trailed out of the room with Elsa who mentioned cook was baking biscuits. That cheered the little girl and she skipped off quite happily.

"Zacharie you promised Millie something we may not be able to deliver. Where on earth can she be talking about?"

"Where is Oliver buried."

"*Cimetière des Grandes Carrières*, how does that help..." then it dawned on her, "...statues and stones with letters carved on them... a graveyard? Surely not? How morbid."

"Perhaps, but it is where he feels closest to his father. He can talk to him, without fear of judgement or admonishment. There is a reason he goes there instead of telling you what troubles him. Hopefully, now we know, he will feel more comfortable sharing those reasons."

"We must not tarry. I do not suppose he thought to wear his coat." Charlotte headed for her bedchamber while Zacharie and Masson went downstairs. Moments later, the three met by the front door, wrapped up against the winter's evening.

The carriage awaited and, mindful of the frigid weather, Masson had organised hot bricks wrapped in thick blankets for their feet. In the gloom, four sure-footed horses, urged on by the driver, trotted briskly through the quiet streets. Fortuitously, the weather had relented although snow continued to drift from laden skies, leaving none in any doubt it would close in again without warning.

The cemetery was not a great distance, but to Charlotte it seemed to take forever. She was all but bouncing off the seat by the time they came to a halt outside the huge wrought iron gate.

"What if it is locked?" She cried, panic overruling the last of her composure.

"Then I shall climb over," Zacharie countered, calmly.

Masson, taking one of the carriage lamps, alighted and, as Zacharie assisted Charlotte out of the coach, he went to check the gate. There was a collective exhale of pent-up breath when it swung open, silently. They followed the winding path to Oliver's grave. Charlotte gripped Zacharie's hand. She was not afraid of the dead, but the strange yellowish-grey twilight cast eerie shadows from the multitude of statues, which, in turn formed ghoulish silhouettes across the ground. How could Noah bear to come here alone? Then she recalled his interest in the catacombs — the cemetery was naught but an open-air version of the same thing.

By now they were within yards of where Oliver was buried. Charlotte nearly whooped with relief when she spotted a figure huddled against the modest yet beautifully carved gravestone. She managed to hold her tongue as the three crept cautiously closer, none wanting to spook the child. When they reached the marble surround of the plot, Charlotte dashed forward and scooped Noah into her arms.

"Noah, my darling, my son, my precious boy, you gave me such a fright. Why did you run away and why here?"

Noah, who was very cold and very sleepy, roused long enough to peer at his mother through heavy-lidded eyes. "Mama? Hello. Papa understands. I'm cold." Was his only reply. His head lolled onto Charlotte's shoulder and he fell back into slumber.

"Permit me to carry him." Zacharie interjected before Charlotte — who was torn between shaking Noah awake to demand an explanation and bursting into tears — could remonstrate with her son. Reluctantly, she relinquished her bundle, admitting he was no lightweight. They hurried back through the ever-increasing darkness, guided by the flickering gleam of the lamp. As soon as they were in the carriage, the driver clicked the reins and the horses lurched forwards, glad to be moving once more.

CHAPTER 14

The journey home passed in the blink of an eye. Noah —
snugly wrapped in a warm blanket on Charlotte's knee,
his feet resting on one of the hot bricks — had not woken again.
Charlotte surmised his breathing was regular and his heart was
beating steadily, if perhaps a little slowly. His body was cold, but
— miracle of miracles — he had thought to wear his winter cloak,
cap, and mittens, so was not as chilled as his mother anticipated.

They were met on their return by anxious staff and a small girl
who was clutching Elsa's hand while jumping up and down. They
paused so Millie could see her brother was safe, then Noah was
whisked upstairs, stripped of his damp clothing and ushered into
a warm bath. A vigorous towelling brought him out of his stupor.
Charlotte got Noah into his nightclothes, after which he was
persuaded to sip some hot chocolate and eat a little of the hearty
broth cook always had bubbling on the stove at this time of the
year. He could not stay awake, however, meaning his explanation
would have to wait until the morning.

Charlotte tucked Noah into bed, and when she dropped a
loving kiss on his forehead, she heard him mumble, "Sorry,
Mama."

"Go to sleep, sweetheart, we'll talk on the morrow." She sat by his bedside, making sure he was properly asleep, and saw a singularly sweet smile cross his lips — so like Oliver's her heart turned over. "I love you, Noah," she whispered.

Elsa came in with a pile of mending. "I'll keep an eye on him, my lady," she assured, "and will come to find you if necessary."

"Thank you, Elsa. Is Monsieur Romain in the library?" Elsa nodded. "Thank you. Goodness, what a day. Now, 'tis time to find Millie and get her to bed too." Smiling at the maid, Charlotte took one last glance at Noah, and left the room. Millie, she discovered was also in the library, sitting on Zacharie's knee, listening to a tale about a snowy rescue. Spying her Mama, Millie flew across the room, slamming into Charlotte's legs. Chuckling, Charlotte lifted her daughter who, in turn, gave her mother a fierce hug.

"Time for bed, poppet," Charlotte said, returning the hug, and scattering kisses over Millie's face making her giggle. "Noah is fast asleep. Tomorrow we might need to have a little talk, the four of us." She met Zacharie's gaze over her daughter's head and he nodded in understanding. "It has been a tiring day; we will all feel much better after a good night's sleep. I shall return momentarily," this last to Zacharie who grinned and resumed his seat, picked up a broadsheet and was immediately engrossed in the latest news.

Charlotte was gone some time, because Millie was inclined to be excitable. It was only by dint of Charlotte reading a story — and when that didn't work, remarking that if she didn't go to sleep, tomorrow would never come — did the child finally settle. Shaking her head at her daughter's slightly flushed cherubic face, she kissed her and said goodnight. Millie was asleep before Charlotte reached the door.

Re-entering the library, Charlotte heaved a contented sigh at the serene ambience. Zacharie, sitting in one of huge wing-back chairs, which circled the fire, was still reading the broadsheet. He had lit his pipe, and the smoke coiled around his head, the aroma not unpleasant. He looked up when she came in. Resting his pipe on its stand, he folded the paper, placed it on the arm of the chair, and stood.

"Both children are asleep, thank goodness," Charlotte moved into his arms, lifting her face for his kiss, which he granted with fervour. While they kissed, the stress of the last few hours dissipated, to be replaced by something just as powerful and far more pleasurable. Breathless, Charlotte broke away, needing him to shed light on an earlier statement, before it slipped her mind. "Zacharie, what did you mean when you said you believed Oliver has given his approval?"

Zacharie leaned back, and stared down at her, grinning at her quizzical expression which made her nose crinkle in the most adorable fashion. "*Mon trésor*, I suspect, if your Oliver disliked me courting you, he would have found a way to make his displeasure known. Perhaps an inexplicably icy draught whenever I am too close to you, or the slap of an invisible hand when I do this..." he kissed her nose.

"You believe in ghosts?"

"I believe in husbands who require reassuring, their wives will be loved wholeheartedly, even when they no longer can."

Charlotte ruminated over this and nodded slowly. To her, although a trifle disquieting, Zacharie's... other-worldly... theory made total sense.

She inhaled a long and steadying breath. There was one more question she dearly wanted to ask but did not wish to seem too forward.

"Zacharie, might I beg a favour?"

"Anything, my love."

Charlotte started to speak, stopped, started again then stepped out of his arms. "'Tis just... I wondered, nay, hoped... that is...

only if you do not... but then perhaps..." she went on in this vein for several minutes until Zacharie, utterly flummoxed, grasped her hand, and tucked her back against his tall frame.

"*Mon ange*, what has you so tongue tied?"

"I would like you to stay, tonight... with me... errr... that is if you might like that too. The rules... and well, children... but still..." she trailed off, embarrassed at her inability to form anything vaguely resembling a sentence. It was quite straightforward, really. Regardless of whether it was proper, or seemly, or acceptable to those who set the rules by which Society ought to abide, she wanted Zacharie with her, in her bed, even if they did nothing more than sleep, and even though they were unwed. The thought of him leaving her alone after today, this day which had gone from heaven to hell and back to heaven again was more than she could bear.

"You want me to stay here with you tonight?" Zacharie needed to be sure. This was not the time to misunderstand. Charlotte nodded, hectic colour flaring up her cheeks. "*Bien sûr, mon amour.* Nothing would give me greater pleasure."

"I know it is audacious, but..."

Zacharie stopped Charlotte's flood of excuses by capturing her mouth with his. He kissed her until she was quite certain her bones were dissolving, and would have slithered to the floor, an ignominy only prevented by Zacharie's strong embrace.

A meal, two glasses of wine and a measure of spirits — brandy for Zacharie, port for Charlotte — later and, after checking on her children twice, Charlotte walked with her betrothed to her bedchamber.

Nerves beset her when the door closed. She did not know whether Zacharie and she would become intimate tonight but, prior to this moment, Oliver was the only man — other than possibly her father when she was a baby — who had seen her naked. She was no longer the willowy young woman she had been when first married; she had borne two children and was approaching her mid-thirties. Yes, she was fit and healthy, and took care of her figure, but…

Once again, she heard Oliver chiding her…

Charlotte, my darling. You have the body of a goddess. I found your curves delectable, far more alluring than a woman who is so thin, her bones slice into you. Stop panicking and bask in the adoration this man is about to pour on you.

Smiling, ruefully, Charlotte walked over to the window, hugging her arms around herself. She heard the light pad of footsteps on the carpet as Zacharie followed her. She tensed, then his arms slid around her, his warm breath caressed her neck, immediately replaced by his lips, causing exquisite shivers to undulate down her spine.

"*Ma chérie*, if this is too soon, I am happy to take my leave," scattering butterfly kisses down her throat. "I have no mind to rush you." His fingers teased along the underside of her arms, make her skin prickle in anticipation.

"I do not want you to go, but this is not as easy as I thought.

"Because of your Oliver?"

"Maybe. He is the only man I have known intimately, and thus the only man…"

"To have seen you naked?"

Charlotte nodded, annoyed with herself for being so… unso-phisticated.

"Firstly, of course Oliver is the only man to have seen you naked, *c'est normal*," Zacharie shrugged — a very Gallic gesture. "So, now I am the second — an honour I am enchanted by, if my lady might swallow her nerves and trust me."

"B-but I am no slender young diamond. I never really was, and since then have given birth, it…" whatever she was going to say was lost as Zacharie stole her words with a sizzling kiss. "Oh," she gasped and almost reeled when he lifted his head.

"Charlotte, *mon amour*, let me love you, let me adore you, let me worship you," his plea, a faint echo of what she imagined Oliver told her to revel in.

"Zacharie..." his name a sigh, which seemed to come from a great distance, and Charlotte gave herself over to his touch.

CHAPTER 15

*I*t was barely dawn when Charlotte awoke the next morning, slowly registering that something heavy was pinning her to the bed, and she was naked... *why was she naked?* About to yell out, her brain caught up, and she recalled the previous night — the weight, an arm slung across her stomach. Instead of a scream, Charlotte's mouth curved in a satisfied smile, as elation suffused her. She rolled onto her side, and the arm slid off her waist, coming to rest at the top of her thigh, in itself enough to spark an ache in her centre.

Raising herself up onto one elbow, Charlotte studied the man lying next to her.

Zacharie was true to his word — he had loved, worshipped and adored her, until she was convinced, she was splintering into a million pieces. Her shyness fled, the instant his lips brushed her shoulder, exposed when — yielding to his insistent fingers — her dress floated to the floor, followed in rapid succession by her gossamer fine undergarments.

Taking Charlotte's hands, Zacharie stood back, and raked a

heated gaze lazily over her body. Charlotte, whose instinct was to cover herself, felt she ought to be embarrassed by the blatant longing in his eyes, but it had the opposite effect. It emboldened her, spurring her to divest him of his clothes with unseemly haste.

That was the only rushed interlude of the night.

Zacharie wove his spell, leisurely and languorously, bringing Charlotte to the peak over and over again, igniting a torrent of sensations — ecstasy, euphoria, rapture — a thirst unquenched until long after the grandfather clock in the hall struck midnight.

As though aware of her scrutiny, Zacharie's captivating eyes flickered open. He smiled, a gentle, loving smile, his hand stroking the silken skin of her leg. She trembled, fire licking along her veins. She stretched up to brush her lips to his.

"Good morning," she murmured against his mouth.

"*Bonjour, mon amour.*" He moved his head and captured her lips, kindling her desire.

Charlotte heard herself moan a plea, uncaring how wanton she sounded. Like a flame to tinder, passion flared — their kiss intensified; tongues tasted, hearts drummed, hands roamed, and limbs entangled.

Sometimes — being lost in love, is where the answers are found.

It being a Saturday, Noah — who appeared none the worse for his snowy escapade — was not required to attend lessons. Just as Charlotte and Zacharie were finishing their belated breakfast, Elsa popped into the dining room to inform Charlotte, both her children were in the nursery.

"I think 'tis time for a discussion with my first born," Charlotte said, wiping her mouth on the pristine napkin, folding it neatly and placing it beside her plate.

"Would you prefer me to absent myself?" Zacharie asked.

Charlotte twisted in her seat to stare at him. "Why on earth should I want that?"

Zacharie spread his palms. "*Ma chérie*, Noah may feel my presence to be inappropriate — given we are not yet wed — perhaps even intimidating. I do not want him to think I am assuming the role of his father. He should be afforded the freedom to accept me in his life, in your life, without coercion. I do not want to begin on… how do you say… the bad toe."

Charlotte chuckled. "The wrong foot, and yes I understand. Nevertheless, I would like us to talk about this as the family we are about to become. Zacharie, we are betrothed, I hope we shall be wed without delay," she blushed at this and fiddled with a knife, lowering her eyes briefly. Cheeks glowing, she raised her head and, fixing him with her gaze, continued. "You are a member of the family now, my love; our marriage merely makes it official. Noah respects you, you have never babied him or spoken condescendingly to him. He talks about you when you are not here, and defers to you when you are, as does Millie. You were the only one who recognised what troubled him — I, his mother, had no idea. Do you not realise? You are already his father and, although it be by choice not blood, 'tis no less important."

She hesitated. *Was an instant family too much for Zacharie to shoulder?* She frowned. It was not as though she had sprung the children on him without warning, they had always been in the picture, but still...

Zacharie noticed the uncertainty cloud her eyes and moved to her side, drawing her out of the chair. "Charlotte, my darling. Nothing thrills me more than becoming husband to you and stepfather to your children and, for me, cannot happen quickly enough. When Millie called me Papa last evening, however inadvertently, I thought my heart would burst with happiness. I just want to tread with caution. Noah is vulnerable at the moment."

"I agree, he is, but there is no time like the present to show we are united in our concern for him," Charlotte paused. "Besides, in truth, I am not confident in my ability to handle this without you. Please." Relieved when he nodded, then kissed her.

"Assuredly, *mon cœur*. Now, let us put poor Noah out of his misery. Doubtless he is anticipating a punishment, *non?*"

"I expect so, and no more than he deserves. His behaviour this last year has been inexcusable, and I admit to being intrigued as to his justification."

The couple strolled through the house and up to the nursery on the second floor. Here, under Elsa's watchful eye, they found Noah playing quietly with his wooden soldiers, and Millie rocking, rather wildly, on Minette — her toy horse — high-pitched giggles testament to how much fun she was having.

"Do be careful, Millie," her mother implored, "too much rocking and Minette might fall over." Reluctantly, Millie slowed the frantic pace and when the rocking came to a stop, climbed down, and ran to her mother.

"Noah, please join us," Charlotte invited. Noah put down the soldier he was holding. Stuffing his hands in his pockets, he approached his mother, perched on the little desk alongside where she was standing, and hung his head. Charlotte glanced at Zacharie and bit her lip to stop herself laughing. Her son was the embodiment of remorse. She pulled up one of the child-sized stools and sat down, facing Noah.

"How are you feeling this morning, sweetheart?" she asked, kindly.

Noah's head shot up, and he examined his mother's face warily. She did not look angry. "I am quite well, thank you," he replied, politely.

"Noah, please tell me what troubles you so deeply, your only recourse was to run away, in the snow, to the cemetery? How do you even know where it is? Is it somewhere you go on a regular basis?"

Noah's gaze slid away, and he shifted from foot to foot. He

wanted to tell Mama, but he was obliged to be stoic and a support. He was the bloody earl. His friends insisted he be strong and let his mother rely on him. He was supposed to look after her, not the other way around — unfortunately, he did not know how.

"Noah," his mother's soft appeal penetrated his thoughts, and his face reddened.

Zacharie sat on the floor and picked up one of the soldiers Noah had been playing with. He studied it for a moment then said, his tone meditative. "When your papa died, I presume your friends were quick to tell you your duties, offering all manner of suggestions. For you are now the earl, with all the responsibilities that entails. Problem is, they really do not know what they are talking about." He saw Noah flinch. Colour drained from the boy's cheeks, leaving a bleached cast to his face, only to darken to crimson again almost instantly. Pretending he hadn't noticed, Zacharie continued without a pause.

"As far as I am aware, not a single one of your friends has lost his father, whether titled or not. Thus, none have been required to assume so arduous a role, neither do they have the slightest knowledge as to what such a role involves. All remain pampered and protected from the trials, life has already thrown at you. Noah, you are very young and not compelled to shoulder the burdens being earl necessitates for another decade. Your papa was so determined you were to be a child for as long as possible, he stipulated… hmmm… wrote it in his will."

CHAPTER 16

$\mathcal{N}$oah gaped at Zacharie and then glanced at his mother, who nodded. "I do not have to care for Mama and Millie? I do not have to sit in parliament, or assist at the embassy, or handle the estate's finances?"

Charlotte fought to smother a grin — now was not the time, but Noah's earnest expression and the litany of responsibilities he expected to undertake at eight years old, was amusing. "No, my precious, not for years and years. Moreover, now I am to marry Zacharie, I think he might like to take care of us all, until you feel ready to assume the title proper. He will probably require a little help here and there... and you know us better than anyone else."

Noah swung his gaze between Charlotte and Zacharie. The oppressive black mass which had been bearing down on him for so many months began to evaporate. "I am sorry, Mama. I did not want to make you sadder and was scared I would be a bad earl. Françoise and Jean kept telling me all the things I ought to be doing, and I knew I was unable to carry out even half of what they described."

"Why did you not come to me, sweetheart?" Charlotte beseeched. "We could have solved this months ago. That you suffered in silence, well, maybe not always in silence..." she arched a brow, her wry expression making Noah chuckle, to his mother's relief, "…is as distressing as losing your Papa."

"They said now I was the earl, I should not keep running to my mother for guidance." Tears brimmed in Noah's eyes. Charlotte groaned and drew her son into a hug. Uncaring that he had long eschewed cuddles, she sat him on her knee and held him close. Finally, the grief Noah had stifled for over a year, poured out. His little body was wracked with sobs and he clung to Charlotte as though he would never let go. This, of course, upset Millie, but Zacharie, spying the tell-tale quiver of her bottom lip diverted her with a quickly invented story about a misunderstood sea-monster.

It was some time before Charlotte was able to calm Noah, who — now he had confessed — could not seem to stop. He told her why he went to his father's grave, that it was the only place he felt able to reveal his woes without fear of reproof. How no one else knew and how he found his way. Noah blurted it all out too fast for total comprehension but Charlotte, wise to childish babble, discerned the general gist. Her heart ached for this little boy who had lost so much yet was afraid to vent his sorrow because of misguided notions fed to him at regular intervals by children who wanted to sound as though they were wiser than he.

Eventually, peace reigned once more. Elsa reappeared, bearing a tray of hot drinks and freshly baked biscuits, which probably did more to brighten spirits than anything else. Noah scrambled off his mother's lap to drag over another stool on which he sat. While they were enjoying their refreshments, Zacharie, with a glance at Charlotte, brought the conversation around to the wedding.

"You know I have asked your Mama to marry me?" There were wide smiles, and nods from the two children. "Well, we have a great favour to beg of you both." Millie and Noah paused, biscuits hovering halfway to their mouths, ever-so slightly tilted heads and quizzical expressions, identical. "Noah, I would be honoured if you would stand with me at the ceremony…"

"…and please will you to do the same for me…" Charlotte asked Millie. "Of course, it *will* mean wearing formal attire, but not for too long."

"What must I do?" Millie piped up.

"All you need to do is stand next to me, when Zacharie and I exchange our vows… errr… say the words which make us husband and wife…" she clarified at Millie's bewildered look. "It is called being a witness and is something only very important people are asked to do. Better still, you may have a new gown." Knowing this would sway her daughter.

"Ohhhh…" Millie clapped her hands, "…what colour?"

"Any colour you like, poppet."

Millie beamed at her mother, and munched the rest of her biscuit, her little face scrunched up in concentration. The colour of her new dress demanded serious consideration.

With Millie otherwise occupied, Charlotte stretched out a hand and pressed Noah's knee. "To stand with Zacharie is your choice, Noah. Please do not feel you *have* to do this, but we wanted to include you in the ceremony, which will be quiet and brief."

"I should be pleased to do so, Mama," her son said after contemplating the offer for a few minutes. "I like Zacharie." His nonchalant praise, oblique approval.

Once all the biscuits had been eaten, and hot chocolate drunk, Millie and Noah scampered off to play. Charlotte watched her children, relieved Noah had finally unburdened himself. She was not naive enough to presume it was all over, that instantaneously he would become the exuberant, light-hearted boy he was prior to his father's death, but it was a start. Now she knew the root cause, hopefully his recovery should be less challenging.

· · ·

Satisfied with what they had achieved thus far, Charlotte rose to her feet and, hooking her arm through Zacharie's, told Noah and Millie she would see them at luncheon. They scarcely noticed the adults' departure, engrossed in childish fun.

"That went rather better than I anticipated," she confided while they headed towards the library. "Are you able to stay or do you have business to which you must attend?"

"I am unencumbered by business until *Mardi*… Tuesday… *ma chérie*. I am, as they say, all yours."

"How delightful. Do you have any suggestions as to how we might fill the days?" Her tone was bland, but when Zacharie spun her to face him, her eyes danced with mischief. Charlotte stared at him for a long moment, reached up, cupped his cheek and grazed her thumb, slowly, along the rim of his bottom lip. "Anything any all?" Her voice might be pure innocence, but her expression beguiled him

Zacharie felt a corresponding throb in that most inconvenient part of his anatomy. "My lady, are you seducing me?"

"Would you like me to?" Her question — part tentative, part provocative.

He gave a wicked grin. "Every day for the rest of our lives, but I want to be the one doing the seducing." Came his immediate reply. A prerogative effectively demonstrated when, in the middle of the hall, and uncaring who might come upon them, Zacharie kissed Charlotte fervently which almost had her begging him to take her right then.

At Charlotte's request, and flouting tradition, to say nothing of those bothersome rules, Zacharie stayed. During the weekend, he moved his few personal effects from the accommodation he rented on the outskirts of the city, to *Maison de Sherbrooke*. On the Sunday afternoon, as they were tidying away the last of his things, Charlotte attempted, in a very circuitous manner, to ascertain whether Zacharie would like his own suite of rooms, aware many of her peers had separate bedchambers.

Astounded, Zacharie gaped, and Charlotte hastened to elaborate.

"Do you wish to sleep alone, *mon amour*, and only share the bed when we make love?" he asked in a sombre tone when she concluded, his face reflecting his puzzlement.

"Only if that is what you prefer." She blushed, twiddling her fingers together. *Goodness this was hard.* She and Oliver had shared a bed throughout their marriage. He had a dressing room, which contained a bed, but the only time he availed himself of it was after she had given birth.

"Do you think I want to sleep without you by my side?"

"I don't… 'tis only that some… I never… until…" Charlotte stopped speaking.

"Charlotte, come now, tell me what is in your heart."

"I want to sleep with you by my side every night and wake up with you every morning. To have you find your own bed after we have been intimate, would make me feel…" she paused again. *How did she articulate what she meant without sounding like a courtesan?*

"Makes you feel what, *mon cœur?*"

"That it was a duty, not a desire." Her words came out in a rush.

Zacharie burst out laughing.

Charlotte frowned. "'Tis not funny," she groused. Her betrothed took her in his arms and peppered her face with kisses, mirth still rumbling in his broad chest.

"Oh, my Charlotte, yes, it is most amusing, *you* are most amusing, but *ma chérie*, please do not chase around the plants when I ask a question. We are to be wed, and ought to be at ease sharing our innermost thoughts, however uncomfortable they occasionally might prove. No, my darling, I absolutely do not want my own rooms. I want to sleep with you every night for as long as the good Lord grants me breath. Even when I am old, and grey, and grumpy, and perhaps a little forgetful, I will still need you next to me, day and night. We have been granted a boon, Charlotte, a second chance at love, and I have no intention of wasting a single moment, even when in slumber."

Relieved, she smiled, a wholly unreserved smile, then flung her arms around him and kissed him back with interest. "Thank goodness," she said some time later, when they got their breath back. "Now, how about a little exercise before it gets dark?" Charlotte squeaked with surprise, when Zacharie swung her into his arms and dropped her on the bed. "I meant a constitutional…" she tried to remonstrate while his fingers made short work of her buttons. "Zacharie…"

Her protest… such as it was… fell on deaf ears.

CHAPTER 17

The gossips among the Paris elite had a field day. Whispers began to circulate that, the recently widowed, Lady Sherbrooke was spurning convention by living with a Frenchman, as though they were *married*... oh, the scandal. This Monsieur Romain was, apparently, a *shipping merchant*... his profession enunciated with disdain accompanied by a well-bred shudder... whose connection to the nobility was tenuous — *quelle horreur*. The rumours even reached London, whereupon someone dared murmur it to Lady Augusta Winchester — purely altruistically, of course — shocked when all she did was smile and remark that it was about time.

Goodness, gracious me, what *was* Society coming to?

Charlotte neither excused nor apologised for her living arrangements. It was her life, her love, her home, and if people were offended by her choices that was their problem, not hers. Zacharie slipped seamlessly into the unruffled hustle and bustle that was everyday life *at Maison de Sherbrooke*.

. . .

On a blustery day in March, a month after Zacharie proposed, the couple was married. The civil ceremony held at the British Embassy — a French official of the State presiding — was followed by a short service in the chapel. The bride and her diminutive witness wore matching gowns in champagne-pink silk, with an overlay in the finest lace, the delicate shade complementing their dark hair to perfection. Zacharie and Noah sported black trousers, charcoal grey jackets and white shirts — their outfits completed by waistcoats and cravats in the palest gold brocade. In deference to Charlotte's status, and to his bride's well-concealed regret, Zacharie — preferring to present a respectable image when he married his love, not the illusion of a sea-faring rogue — had trimmed his hair.

Noah *was* heard to complain that his cravat tickled, and Millie *was* inclined to skip or dance instead of walk, but otherwise both children behaved impeccably.

The wedding breakfast was also hosted by the embassy and, when the offer was made, Charlotte wondered whether this was somewhat imprudent. Was it fair to Zacharie, being wined and dined in the same rooms where Oliver spent most of his days? Would it be too poignant a reminder of her dead spouse? The attaché took pains to convince her, that in recognition of the tireless efforts of the late earl, they would be honoured to provide this banquet — and it was indeed a banquet — for their esteemed Lady Sherbrooke and her groom.

Zacharie, with the typical superstition of a sailor, assured his beloved that if Oliver wanted to haunt him, it would be far more likely to happen in the bedchamber than in his old offices. Oliver himself was quiet — Charlotte rarely heard his voice anymore. He would always be with her… in her memories, in the faces of their children… but she no longer needed his reassurance, even if it was only ever a fantasy fabricated by her bereaved mind.

A day which might have become emotional for all the wrong

reasons, was one full of merriment and cheer. Those in attendance declared how wonderful it was to share the celebrations of
so happy a couple.

~

Charlotte intended to adopt her husband's surname, as protocol
dictated. Even though this was the convention, Zacharie tried to
persuade her to retain Sherbrooke… asserting she was still the
countess and, furthermore, Sherbrooke was a venerable title.
Until Noah married, she ought to keep it. Charlotte, well-versed
in the hereditary tenets of the peerage, disagreed. This resulted in
a mildly heated debate, which ended abruptly when Zacharie
hauled his wife against him and kissed her soundly.

"Zacharie, you cannot solve every disagreement with a kiss,"
Charlotte gasped while batting at him — to little effect.

"Oh, I think I probably can," Zacharie alleged, and kissed her
again, just to prove his point.

Silence fell as their ardour rose, and Charlotte, despite being
adamant this was not the end of the discussion, conceded her
husband was correct. He would win her over every single time
with this technique. At the back of her mind, Charlotte knew she
ought to feel irked at how readily she capitulated, but quite
honestly, she relished it... and — a wicked imp inside whispered
— she could use it to her advantage.

"Fine," she granted, breathlessly when, eventually, he relinquished her lips, "I will agree to keep Sherbrooke, if you will
agree to a compromise."

Zacharie's brow rose quizzically, and he kissed her nose.
"Which is…"

"That I have both names. *Mon chéri*, I am proud to be your
wife, I want the world to know you are my husband. I also
acknowledge your contention the Sherbrooke title is important.
Henceforth, and until Noah weds, I will be Lady Charlotte
Romain, Countess of Sherbrooke. This way I honour you and

Oliver. Indulge me, my love." Her fingers found their way around his back, seeking under his waistcoat to tweak his shirt from his trousers and skim over warm flesh.

Zacharie sucked in a breath.

"Are we in accord?" she murmured against his mouth, shamelessly exploiting her feminine wiles.

"Not fair! How can I argue when you are driving me to distraction," he rasped, his body pulsing in response to his wife's provocation.

"Oh, I think this is easily as fair as you kissing me into submission." She gurgled with laughter. "I repeat, are we in accord?"

"I surrender, *ma petite séductrice*." Zacharie chuckled at her mischievous expression.

"Prove it," she entreated, her voice catching, her fingers tiptoeing lower.

Thankful they were alone in their bedchamber, and unlikely to be disturbed, Zacharie did just that.

When spring broke through winter's clutches, Zacharie suggested they journey to London. He and Hugh Drummond were about to conduct, what could prove to be lengthy business negotiations. He did not want to be apart from Charlotte any longer than necessary, and it would give them all the chance to re-establish their bond with family in England. Charlotte was excited at the prospect, and thus, several days of frantic packing, unpacking, and repacking ensued. Letters were sent, and the staff at *Maison de Sherbrooke* were apprised of their employers' imminent departure.

"We hope to return before summer, Masson," Charlotte said, after explaining the reasons for what might seem a precipitous decision.

"We shall keep the house in readiness." He bowed, smiling.

"Thank you, Masson. I do not know what I would do without

you." Uncaring how it might look to others, she took the elderly man's hand and squeezed it lightly. "You have been my rock this past eighteen months and I am truly grateful."

"It has, and will continue to be, my pleasure, *ma dame*." His shrewd blue eyes twinkled. Lady Charlotte Romain was a treasure, and he defied anyone to contradict him.

Charlotte grinned and, after apologising for interrupting his duties — which made him chuckle, ran up the stairs, with scant disregard for her status, calling for Noah and Millie.

A sunny Monday in April saw a family of four disembarking at the Trentams~Romain docks, to a welcome fit for royalty. Those of Charlotte's family who could be there, were, as was Zacharie's aunt, whom Helena had tracked down to her comfortable manor house near Dorchester. Zacharie's surprise and broad smile, worth the hours it took Helena to persuade Lady Emsworth that her nephew would be delighted to see her after so many years.

It was a bitter-sweet reunion. Only three members of Charlotte's family had seen her since Oliver's death, and although they, as well as Hugh, knew and liked Zacharie, the remainder had never met him. In the space of a few moments they had to both console and congratulate. Thankfully, the Winchester and Drummond families were nothing if not inclusive. Zacharie was greeted with open arms — literally — grinning at his wife's... 'well you know we are a family who love to hug' ...as he was swallowed into yet another embrace.

Augusta had invited them to stay with her at Winchester House for the duration of their time in London and thus, the Sherbrooke city residence remained closed. If plans changed, Charlotte would arrange for it to be opened, but for now, Zacharie and she were glad not to have the extra responsibility. Noah and Millie were thrilled to see their grandmama, a sentiment wholly reciprocated.

For the first week or so, Charlotte and Zacharie were caught up in a seemingly never-ending round of social calls, which was as exhausting as it was entertaining. It did threaten to become overwhelming, and Zacharie admitted to being relieved when his business commitments limited his participation. Charlotte used this, as well as the fact they were newly-weds as an excuse to refuse many subsequent invitations.

All in all, however they began to settle into London life.

CHAPTER 18

*O*nce Zacharie and Hugh's negotiations were concluded, the Sherbrooke-Romain family travelled to the Sherbrooke country seat in rural Wiltshire. On the way, they spent a week at Whiteoaks, the Winchester family home in Hampshire. Millie and Noah had a marvellous time playing around the vast estate, with Max, Vivienne, and Thea — Billie and Giles' three children. Their numbers augmented, more often than not, by Beatrice and Hannah — Theo and Grace Elliott's two daughters, as well as Kate and Freddy — Jessica and Duncan Barrington's youngsters.

The air rang with childish laughter and chatter. Noah and Max, who were rapt to discover they were the same age, led the others into all manner of mischief. At the end of every day they all tumbled into their respective homes, usually grubby, quite frequently wearing half the garden but, without exception, supremely happy. Noah, particularly, was in his element, reverting to the cheerful, carefree boy he used to be. All this made Charlotte ponder the wisdom of returning to Paris permanently. Yes, she accepted this sojourn was out of the ordinary, but spending time with her family reminded Charlotte of a half-formed wish, the day she begged Zacharie's advice about Noah's tantrums. To come back and live in England was a much more attractive proposition than it had been to date, and something on which she valued Zacharie's opinion.

When they reached Sherbrooke Hall, Charlotte mentioned her dilemma to her husband, whereupon they discussed it in depth. Zacharie had no preference, wherever Charlotte wanted to live he would be content — *she* was his home, not the building, or country in which they resided. Their conversation went around and around. They came up with and discarded several ideas, and an answer seemed frustratingly remote… that was until Zacharie offered a tantalising solution.

"*Mon amour*, perhaps we consider dividing our year between Paris and London, say three or four months in each centre, and adjustable should events dictate. I have the company in Dieppe, I must be in France for some portion of every year, but I also have commitments in London." He shrugged, in his quintessentially Gallic manner. "I believe this gives us… hmmm… *le meilleur des deux mondes… oui?*" At Charlotte's uncomprehending look, he clarified, "I think you say… the better of the two worlds… *mais, tout ce que tu veux ma chérie, je suis content…* but, I am content with whatever you want, my darling." He translated. "We will work it out to suit ourselves, *n'est-ce pas?*"

"You are very French all of a sudden," Charlotte teased with a grin. "No, please don't stop," when her husband's brow creased, thinking she was making fun of him. "I love to hear you speaking French. It is most definitely the language of romance, of love…" she paused, then all but purred, "…of seduction."

Zacharie began murmuring in his mother tongue, interspersing each word with a kiss. Charlotte, familiar quivers beginning to thrum down her spine, quickly succumbed to his verbal temptation.

"This is not getting us any closer to a decision," she husked.

"I beg to disagree," Zacharie growled.

"How so," her voice catching when his lips trailed down her throat.

"These are all the reasons we ought to retain our home in Paris."

"Do I need to know what they are?"

"Not right at this moment… perhaps later." Unwilling to admit some of his list included an inventory of equipment installed on ships. What his wife did not understand, she could not hold against him.

Charlotte — not *entirely* incognisant of the French language, and who caught the words for rope and sail — smiled a secret smile, kept her counsel, and allowed Zacharie to think he'd won that debate too.

April quickly became May, and the family savoured their time at Sherbrooke Hall, the gentle Wiltshire countryside lulling them with its tranquility. Zacharie and Charlotte dealt with any outstanding estate matters, which turned out to be minimal — the manager and stewards, Oliver hired so long ago, had proved their worth. Everything was as it should be, and Charlotte was satisfied the Sherbrooke assets were in trustworthy hands. Noah's inheritance was safe.

It was not all business. Charlotte wanted to show Zacharie and the children as much of Wiltshire as she could, and they had great fun exploring the surrounding area. Salisbury was a favourite, especially the cathedral. Noah took great satisfaction in comparing it with the Church of *Ste-Geneviève*, declaring he preferred Salisbury. That the latter boasted the tallest spire and the oldest working clock in Britain might have been the deciding factors.

Stonehenge, on Salisbury Plain and recently purchased by the Antrobus family, was another fascinating site. Charlotte called upon Sir Edmund, the current baronet, who, dazzled by the beautiful countess, gladly granted her permission to take her family around the henge. In the event, he offered to escort them and proved to be quite knowledgeable about the somewhat perplexing circle of monoliths virtually in his back garden, so to speak.

The baronet's visitors were gratifyingly astonished by the ancient standing stones, and Zacharie kept them all enthralled with tales of Merlin who, according to folklore, was the architect of the henge. The adults were not entirely sure a shadowy figure of myth did indeed magic the stones all the way from Ireland, but it made for a great story.

In the opposite direction from Stonehenge was the Cherhill White Horse. Although a little further afield than most of the other places they ventured to, one of the stewards had assured them the extra distance was worth it. None had seen this or any other 'white horse' before and were intrigued by what to expect. As the name suggested, it turned out to be a huge rendering of a horse, cut into the chalk hillside. Designed by a Dr Alsop — who was by all accounts, rather eccentric — the stark white of the figure stood out against the lush green grass and was visible long before you reached the base of the slope into which it was carved. Noah, with all the importance of being eight, led Millie right around the edge, adjuring his sister not to slip off the grass onto the glittering white chalk. Millie declared Cherhill was nearly as much fun as *le jardin des Tuileries,* her comment making Charlotte smile in reminiscence.

They visited Malmesbury Abbey, where Charlotte pointed out the marks left by gun shot. Malmesbury was subject to fierce battles and changed hands several times during the Great Civil War, over two centuries earlier, the abbey bearing the brunt of the fighting.

That sent Noah in search of stray bullets, Millie tagging along, his willing helper — a hunt which kept the two occupied for hours.

In between these jaunts the four relaxed at Sherbrooke. The sprawling, yet beautifully apportioned Hall had always been a haven for Charlotte and Oliver, particularly during the long parliamentary recess. They spent the majority of every summer in this idyllic backwater, untroubled by whatever else was happening in Society.

One morning, while the children were playing in the gardens — under Elsa's supervision — Charlotte asked Zacharie to help her put Oliver's personal effects and clothes into storage. Thus far, the bedchamber she shared with her first husband had remained closed. Her present marital status made no difference, even if still a widow, Charlotte could not have slept there… it was imbued with too many memories.

"I realise this sounds like a peculiar request, and please say no if you think it inappropriate. I do not want you to feel uncomfortable," she tried to explain her motives to Zacharie, when she broached the subject, "but it is as though by helping me you will understand a little of who Oliver was. I cannot tell you *why* it is important to me that you know, it just is."

"Do not fret, my love. I am not troubled by Oliver. I have the impression he was a good man. How else could he have engendered such love from his wife and children and been so well respected among his peers. As I have said before, if Oliver was displeased with me, I would not be married to you."

Which, of course, earned him a heartfelt kiss.

"This bedchamber will be Noah's," Charlotte elaborated, sometime later when they entered the silent room. The furniture was covered in huge cloth sheets, and the curtains drawn. Charlotte walked over to the closest window and flung back the heavy drapery, blinking in the dazzling sunshine which poured through and coughing at the cloud of dust which rose from the material.

"Tsk, this room needs airing and cleaning," she groused.

"Doubtless, the staff have been awaiting your instructions regarding this room, *mon amour*. They would not presume to enter the room of a dead earl without permission. 'Tis not done."

"Fair point, but now we are here, it should be attended to. Once we have finished this task, I will ask them to spring clean it and keep it in a state of readiness."

The rest of the day was spent sifting through the belongings of a dead man. Charlotte found one or two precious treasures she could not bear to part with, and Zacharie had no objections — he was not in competition with a ghost. Moreover, this was thirteen years of her life, a life he knew nothing of, and Charlotte was the women he loved *because* of Oliver. In truth, Zacharie was indebted to the earl. Without him, it was likely he would be a committed bachelor, still mourning for Nathalie, instead of being entranced every waking moment by a raven-haired bewitching beauty who could turn his head to mush and his body to a raging inferno with barely a smile.

He studied Charlotte as she pottered about the room deciding what ought to be kept, or could be feasibly given away, or thrown out.

She glanced across and saw him watching her. His inscrutable expression causing a frown to mar her brow. "Is this too hard, *mon cœur*? How thoughtless I am. 'Tis wrong, nay cruel, of me to entreat my new love to help me say goodbye to my old."

In three strides, Zacharie was by her side. "Non, *ma belle*, I am honoured you trust me to share this task. I was just thinking how grateful I am to your Oliver.

Charlotte angled her head and pinned him with an inquisitive grey gaze. "Grateful? That seems an… unorthodox sentiment."

"Without him, my darling, I would not be the happiest man in

Christendom. I would be a humble shipping merchant living in rented rooms, existing from day to day. Not happy not sad, just resigned and with little to look forward to. By the grace of God, and although in grievous circumstances, I met you and my bleak future has become one of unqualified bliss." His lips grazed her forehead.

Her cheeks blooming a becoming pink, Charlotte replied. "I confess, when Oliver died, my world collapsed. I did not think the sun would ever shine again, or that the birds would continue to sing, or flowers to blossom. To fall in love again, to find another man who would capture my heart and soul so completely was inconceivable. I often wonder whether it was Oliver who guided you to me. I used to fancy I heard him encouraging me when I faltered, or when I doubted whether I dared believe in an acquaintance which was growing into something more enduring. Fate is curious. The last thing you expect, becomes the one thing you never want to live without."

"Curious she may be. Unpredictable? Definitely. But who are we to argue with destiny?"

"I never argue," Charlotte contended.

"I beg to differ, *mon ange*, but in this instance, I shall let it slide."

"Oh, how generous, monsieur. I am the epitome of a compliant wife, never a cross…"

"Who are you trying to convince?" he grinned, interrupting her indignation. "Hush and let me see just how compliant you are."

Which he did, most effectively.

CHAPTER 19

*P*aris — *February 1828*

Zacharie Romain was pacing the floor of the library — the rug in front of the fire would likely never recover from his continuous footfall. Noah and Millie were with their cousins, uncle, and grandmother in the drawing room. Charlotte was in the bedchamber.

When his wife told him she was increasing, Zacharie's initial reaction was of unmitigated joy, immediately followed by an almost crippling terror. Nathalie died in childbirth and she had been a young, healthy woman of one and twenty. Charlotte was healthy, but she was five and thirty... much older than the age considered even relatively safe for birthing a child. Charlotte, wise to his fears did everything in her power to soothe his dread. Her pregnancy was generally untroubled, and once the sickness passed, she glowed.

Following a protracted sojourn in England, where Charlotte

sought the advice of specialists, recommended by Theo Elliott — her brother's best friend — they returned to Paris in the autumn. Docteur Allard, apprised of her condition, visited every week to ensure even the slightest problem was not missed. Zacharie was inclined to wrap his wife in cotton wool, but Charlotte refused to be coddled. She was careful, and continued her life as though nothing had changed, although she did decide, attending the children's hospital during this period would be imprudent. Now she had come to term, and Zacharie had never felt more powerless.

A knock at the door broke into his reverie and had him spinning around. He saw Billie — who, husband and children in tow, had travelled with Augusta to assist at the birth — peek her head around.

"Zacharie she is asking for you."

"You will allow me to be with her?"

Billie grinned. "I have no say in the matter. Charlotte has demanded your presence, because, as she so succinctly put it, 'tis your fault she is in such discomfort."

Zacharie grinned sheepishly, then bounded out of the room and up the stairs to their bedchamber. On their bed, his wife was cursing up a storm. At any other time, her expletives would have made him laugh, she often astounded him with her colourful language, not so today.

"Zacharie? Is that you? Get yourself over here. You got me in this predicament, you will bloody well stay until I am out of it."

He sank into the chair beside the bed and grasped her hand, tucking errant strands of hair off her face. Even in the throes of agony, Charlotte took his breath away. "*Mon amour,* I am here. I wish I could bear the pain for you, but I cannot."

"The devil, Zacharie. I, erroneously by the way, assumed it got easier. This is my third child and 'tis more agonising than the first." She lifted her head and glared at him. "I want to hate you, but I cannot. I love you, *mon chéri.* Should anything happen…" Despite Charlotte's outward confidence, she was not wholly able to disguise her anxiety. She knew the risks associated with childbirth.

A trace of Charlotte's underlying trepidation lurked in the stormy hue of her eyes, adding to his own dread. Zacharie's heart clenched, but he strove to sound positive. "Nothing will happen, my darling. You have the midwife, and Billie, and I will not leave you.

"Noah and Millie?"

"Are with your Mama. Fret not, *mon trésor*, focus on me." Zacharie launched into a nonsensical monologue about goodness knows what, speaking in French for he knew the musical lilt soothed his wife. Their eyes locked. Charlotte was convinced the love flowing from Zacharie's forest-green gaze was a tangible thing, and she drew strength from its power. The contractions were coming very close together now and, while trying to follow the midwife's instructions, as well as remembering to breathe, Charlotte concentrated on her husband, who reckoned she might break his hand, she gripped it so tightly.

After what, to Charlotte and Zacharie, was surely hours, there was a triumphant cry from the midwife and a lusty squall from the minute individual who had just been expelled, unceremoniously, into the world. Bathed in sweat, panting heavily, and flushed deep red, Charlotte — shuddering with relief — stared at Zacharie, the hint of a weary smile beginning to form.

Before too long, Billie carried over the newborn, swaddled in a soft blanket. "May I present your son?" She placed the bundle in Charlotte's waiting arms.

Charlotte tweaked the cloth and gazed into the face of her child. A rush of emotion engulfed her, and she could not prevent the tears from spilling over.

Zacharie was in awe. With one gentle finger he stroked the infant's cheek. He leaned over and kissed Charlotte, murmuring for her ears only. "Charlotte Romain, *mon amour*, you are my heart, my life, my world, thank you for so priceless a gift."

She reached out and grasped his hand. "Zacharie Romain, *je t'aime, je t'adore*, and you are so very welcome." She lay against the pillows, drained and desperate for sleep, but then the midwife caused a sensation.

"No need to be resting yet, my sweet, the next one will be needing a bit of a push."

There was an immediate and stunned silence.

Charlotte and Zacharie wore identical expressions of stupefaction.

"Pardon me, the next one?" Charlotte croaked.

"The other baby will be here momentarily." In a tone indicating they really ought to have known this.

Charlotte swung her gaze towards the door as though expecting someone to appear with another child. "I apologise for seeming confused. I am only having one baby."

"Non, *ma petite*, you are having twins. Did the physician not inform you?"

"Twins?" Zacharie wheezed, his brain refusing to process the midwife's words.

Charlotte continued to gape slack-jawed, words — not unexpectedly, but quite understandably — failing her. "Do we look as though he informed us?" She eventually stammered. Closing her eyes, Charlotte tried, in vain, to recall everything Docteur Allard had said over the last few months, any pertinent comments she had misinterpreted. She shook her head in the hope she was dreaming, but when she opened them, nothing had changed. Billie gathered the newborn from his mother's arms, assuring Charlotte he would be in the crib. The midwife fussed about, then the contractions started again.

Charlotte groaned, uncertain she possessed the stamina or courage to deliver another baby. "Leave it there, I cannot do this today. I need to sleep." She wailed.

"Yes, you can my love." Zacharie coaxed. "Look at me."

Charlotte did as her husband bid, seeing not only her dishevelled reflection, but also the depths of his devotion in the vivid green of his eyes. She gritted her teeth.

"Breathe, just keep breathing." Zacharie forced aside his panic. Charlotte needed him. She was so pale, her breathing was coming in agonised gasps, her skin was clammy, and her eyes were glazed.

"I am too tired," she whimpered.

"Nearly there," Billie encouraged, "You *can* do this, Charlotte. You are stronger than any woman I know."

To which, Charlotte let loose a string of oaths, then apologised — to the amusement of her listeners.

"No need to apologise." Billie grinned. "Swear all you like, just remember to push when I ask."

To Zacharie, it seemed as though an eon had passed before a sharp cry echoed around the room.

"Is that it? Am I done? Please do not make me have any more. If there are any more, they can wait, maybe for a year or two." Charlotte closed her eyes, sucking in lungsful of air, still clutching Zacharie's hand like a lifeline.

Billie came over with another bundle. She placed the child in Zacharie's arms, aware Charlotte was fading. "You have a beautiful daughter."

Zacharie stared at the precious scrap of humanity, his eyes filled with tears. He lifted his gaze to Charlotte who was watching him through drooping lids. "My darling, she is perfect."

"Good… good… that is sooooooo…" her words trailed off and she slid into oblivion.

"Charlotte!" Zacharie virtually leapt out of the chair, forgetting he had an infant in his arms. Panic that he was going to lose her even now, clawing at him.

"Hush, you great lug, she is sleeping. See her chest moves steadily." The midwife tutted, comfortingly… *this is why husbands should not be with their wives during childbirth… too easily panicked. Her ladyship insisted and this tiny countess agreed — so who was she to argue, but still, tsk...* while busily doing whatever else was required.

Zacharie, who had no mind to know what was happening at that end of the bed, kept his eyes on Charlotte's face, watching for the slightest sign she was waking, or something was wrong.

Billie, aware of Zacharie's consternation, walked across the room to stand behind him. Resting her hand on his shoulder she said placatingly. "Charlotte will be fine, the births were not too complicated — gruelling and of course painful, but your wife did marvellously. She needs rest and plenty of cosseting. Twins... bless me but you two never do things by halves do you?" Billie chuckled, squeezed his shoulder, and went to assist the midwife. "I will tell Mama and the children," she added, bundling up the bloodied sheets ready to be burned.

Zacharie, rocking his daughter and observing his wife, would never be able to describe the deluge of emotions which had cascaded through him during the last however many hours. He was so proud of Charlotte, his heart was about ready to burst out of his chest. His fear lingered; Charlotte was not out of danger, but he trusted Billie, so banked it down and concentrated on the babies. Being party to so wondrous a creation, both astounded and flummoxed him, but the love which swelled when he first saw his new son and daughter would never wane, and he knew he would die to protect them.

CHAPTER 20

An hour or so later, Charlotte stirred. Momentarily baffled as to why she was sore and ached all over. Then it flooded back, she was mother to twins… heavens, that was a facer. She began to smile.

"Charlotte, *mon amour.*"

She turned her head to see Zacharie sitting by the bed. He was cradling one of their babies, and it was an image she would never forget. Her husband's face, though tired, seemed lit from within, his expression one of stunned reverence as he gazed at her.

"Zacharie, our babies are healthy?"

"They are both healthy, possess the requisite number of fingers and toes… which are the most adorable things you ever saw, by the way… and, I am glad to say, look just like their bewitching Mama. They already have me wound around their thumbs." He reached out and grasped Charlotte's hand. "Would you like to hold our daughter?"

Charlotte, her mouth twitching at Zacharie's interpretation of the English idiom, nodded and tried to shuffle up the pillows, huffing in frustration. Everything was such an effort.

Billie, who had been sitting by the fire in case she was required, came over to help. "That more comfortable?" she asked, plumping up the pillows and tucking another couple behind Charlotte to prop her up.

"Yes, thank you, Billie."

"'Tis some time since you had any sustenance and, although a large meal would be too much, how about a cup of my sweet tisane, and perhaps a little something to eat?"

"That would be lovely, I am rather hungry." Charlotte replied, realising it was probably over twelve hours since her last meal. Billie bustled off, leaving husband and wife with their new-borns.

"Goodness me, twins! How are we going to do this?" Charlotte looked at Zacharie, wide-eyed, as he passed her their daughter, and then scooped their son out of his crib.

"With humour and patience, I suspect," Zacharie replied, with a grin. "How do you feel, my love?"

"Sore and fatigued, although both are strangely eliminated by the most blissful euphoria. 'Tis a sentiment, I hope, never fades. I love you, Zacharie. Thank you for being with me and I am sorry I cursed you."

Laughter rumbled through Zacharie's chest, and he brushed his lips to her forehead. "I love you more, and do not think on it. I do not know how you women do this." He waved a hand between them over the babies, his inference obvious. "Your strength and endurance astonish me. I am humbled in the face of such courage."

"*Mon cœur*, any courage came from knowing you were by my side, I would have given up if not for you. Now the biggest question is what are we going to call these angels?"

Despite having nine months to prepare, thus far, they had not been able to agree on any names. If they had a boy, Charlotte wanted to name him Édouard, after Zacharie's father, and for a girl, Yvette — the name Zacharie and Nathalie had chosen if their child was a daughter. Zacharie had suggested Oliver to honour her first husband and he wanted Charlotte to be one of the names they bestowed on a daughter. They did both like the name Sophia, which had no connection to either family, but otherwise, neither was wholly comfortable with the other's suggestions and so all they had reached was an impasse.

"Perhaps we need to live with them for a day or two before we decide. We want names which will suit them not us," Zacharie posited.

"What a splendid idea. I am too tired to think now anyway," Charlotte smiled. "Do Noah and Millie know?

"Billie told them, but I expect they might like to see you and the babes. Could you cope with a very quick visit?"

"Yes please…" Balancing her daughter in one arm, Charlotte reached out and took her husband's hand, squeezing it gently, words unnecessary.

Noah and Millie managed to contain their excitement, but their beaming smiles and the little jigs they gave when they saw the twins, were evidence enough. Augusta sat with Charlotte for a few minutes and proclaimed herself overjoyed to be a grand-mother again. Mother and daughter chatted desultorily, but Charlotte was finding it hard to focus and Augusta, wise to such fatigue, slipped quietly away when Billie returned with a platter of food.

In between visitors, Charlotte ate and drank enough to satisfy Billie, but she was tiring and, by the time Zacharie came back into their room after being dispatched to eat a decent meal, Charlotte was nodding off. While Zacharie was absent, the midwife had taken the opportunity to examine her patient and wash her properly. Then she, with the assistance of Billie, Elsa and Berthe, changed the bed linens before helping Charlotte into a fresh nightgown, brushed and plaited her hair, and wrapped a warm woollen shawl around her shoulders.

The babies were snug in their crib, fortunately big enough to accommodate two for now, although Zacharie made a mental note to commission a second one the following day.

Zacharie's intent was to sleep in one of the guest rooms,

where a bed had been made up for him. Charlotte was having no such thing

"Please stay," she murmured, drowsily. "Tonight, of all nights I need you next to me."

"My darling, you have been through an arduous ordeal, you need space and privacy not some great length of a man hogging the bedclothes," in reference to Charlotte's contention that every time he turned over, he took all the covers with him.

"I only ever rest peacefully with you beside me. I am the invalid here, so you must pander to my every whim." Her eyes opened seeking his, and her exhausted grey gaze daring him to defy her.

"Charlotte Romain you are a stubborn minx and no mistake. Fine…" when it looked as though she was going to upbraid him, "…you win, I will not argue with a brand-new mother. I value my own health." He winked at her, shrugged out of his clothes, and pulled on a night-shirt. With one last look at the babies — who were deep in slumber — he eased, cautiously, into bed. Charlotte turned and, moulding herself to him, nestled her head into the crook of his neck, and slung her arm across his waist. Zacharie drew up the covers, kissed her shining hair and closed his eyes.

When Billie popped in half an hour later to check on mother and twins, Charlotte and Zacharie were fast asleep. She smiled to herself, glad all was well, although she would never forget the dumbfounded looks on the faces of both parents when informed they were about to have a second baby. The smile became a grin and she stored it away to tell Giles — who had been doing a sterling job entertaining five children — when she too sought her bed.

Within an hour, *Maison de Sherbrooke* was enveloped in darkness, the only sound, the gentle breathing of a household at rest.

EPILOGUE

LATE MARCH 1828

A crisp, sunny morning in Paris. A fleet of coaches rattled away from the front of a classically elegant house on *rue d'Anjou*. A family stood on the pavement waving madly. Two adults, each holding a tiny bundle, were rather more restrained than the two young children who were jumping up and down next to them, shouting goodbye, their treble voices loud in the cool, still air. They stood until the coaches turned onto the *rue du Faubourg Saint Honoré* and disappeared out of sight. With a sigh, Charlotte Romain spun around and climbed the few steps to their front door. The other three following on her heels.

Masson closed the door and Charlotte leaned against it, resting her head on the polished wood while absently patting the blanket covered back of the infant snuggled into her shoulder.

"Thank you, Masson, for everything these last few weeks. I know you have been sorely tested with so many extra people in the house, but you and the staff have, as ever, surpassed yourselves."

"Think nothing of it my lady, it has been most pleasant hosting your family."

Charlotte chuckled. "I think that is the politest way to put it, monsieur. Hopefully, life will revert to its usual state of organised confusion."

Masson grinned and bowed, departing to attend to his duties

~

In the weeks since the birth of the twins, chaotic was the best way to describe life at *Maison de Sherbrooke*. The upheaval created by six extra family members, and two new babies, had turned the normally quiet house into something resembling a battlefield. Five children running amok, and infant twins who were learning to drown out everyone else when they were hungry, or tired, or needed changing, meant the walls all but reverberated with a din which only ceased when the children were in bed. Even then the nights were disturbed when the twins demanded attention.

As she had with both Noah and Millie, Charlotte fed the babies herself — eschewing a wet nurse. It was rewarding if not a little restrictive, but she would not have it any other way. Charlotte knew nursing strengthened their bond, not to mention it was the most convenient way to feed them and helped her own body heal faster.

Zacharie and Charlotte finally agreed on names for the twins, a decision in which Fate, once again — if somewhat indirectly — took a hand.

Charlotte was moving some of Noah and Millie's things from the nursery into their bedrooms, to make room for the plethora of gifts lavished on the twins from family in England. One such item was an anthology of ancient myths and legends, gifted to Millie upon her birth by Oliver's parents who, sadly, had died shortly thereafter — within six months of one another. Charlotte remembered Oliver commenting that it was a book he loved when a child. It was a huge tome, the cover creased with age and, despite the content being rather beyond Millie's comprehension, the little girl cherished it. Recalling how many times she had read to her daughter from this book, Charlotte sat down and opened the cover. The first thing she saw was the dedication inscribed on the fly leaf.

To our adored granddaughter, Millicent, in celebration of your birth.

This book belonged to your great grandmama, for whom you are named, and who would want you to have it.

Magical adventures await you inside, and we hope you find it as enthralling as she did.

Remember Millicent, you are limited only by your imagination.

With our deepest affection,

Grandpapa Philip and Grandmama Olivia

Charlotte mused over the dedication, belatedly realising Oliver was almost certainly named for his mother — she had not given the similarities in their names much thought before. Taking the book, she tracked Zacharie to the study, where he was buried up to his elbows in paperwork. He stood when she entered, greeting her with a quick yet passionate kiss.

"To what do I owe this pleasure, *mon ange?*"

"I think I have an idea for the twins' names." Charlotte went on to explain what she had just read. "Perhaps we might name our son Philippe Édouard Zacharie, and our daughter Sophia Olivia Charlotte. Both Noah and Millie have three names. They include those of my parents and, as this dedication indicates, Millie is named for her great grandmama. I know it seems excessive, but we only ever use one. It pleased both of our families immensely, and to be honest, was actually easier than trying to choose one or two for each of them. In the same way, we honour your father and Oliver, but less overtly. For every day, they would be simply Philippe and Sophia Romain…" Charlotte let her suggestion hang.

Trying to decide what to call their precious twins was the

closest they ever came to a real argument and Charlotte, who never backed down from heated debate whatever the topic, was tired of offering solutions to the stalemate. Moreover, there was the not insignificant matter of the christening, less than three days hence. Time was of the essence.

"The inspiration for these names came from a book?" Zacharie wanted to clarify Charlotte's choice, spying the hint of weariness flicker across his wife's face. He too wanted the issue of names resolving. Calling them baby boy and baby girl, although amusing at first, was becoming tedious.

"No, it was the dedication. Here look…" she put the book on the desk and opened it, showing Zacharie the flyleaf.

He read the beautiful copperplate writing, then asked, curiously. "What prompted you to look at this particular book."

Charlotte shrugged, "I didn't. I was taking it from the nursery to Millie's bedroom and something made me glance through it. It fell open here and the names struck a chord. They sound lovely together, they roll off the tongue like a melody." She smiled up at her handsome husband. "Try it."

Zacharie did so and had to agree. "There is only one way to know for certain. Come." He grasped Charlotte's hand and led her upstairs to where the twins were, hopefully, fast asleep. Proud parents stood shoulder to shoulder and gazed down at the tiny babies.

"Philippe Édouard Zacharie Romain," Charlotte murmured. Their son stretched and snuffled but did not wake.

"Sophia Olivia Charlotte Romain," Zacharie intoned just as quietly. Their daughter's eye-lids fluttered, and she opened them, to stare at the two faces hovering above her. Her little mouth formed what Charlotte swore was a smile even though she knew in truth it was probably wind, then drifted back to sleep.

"I think our decision is made, *mon amour*. If that is not tacit approval, I do not know what is." He grinned and drew Charlotte into his arms. "I would like to demonstrate how highly I approve, and it may not be so silent."

"What did you have in mind, Monsieur Romain," Charlotte asked innocently, while an impish smile twitched at her lips.

"'Tis easier if I show you, than waste time explaining." He put a finger to his lips, and they crept out of the nursery. Zacharie led his wife along to their bedchamber, the fire in the hearth taking the chill out of the room, but the warmth was paltry compared with the heat licking along Charlotte's veins as her husband demonstrated, most effectively, exactly what he meant.

~

That was five days ago. The christening, at the chapel attached to the embassy was well attended, and afterwards at *Maison de Sherbrooke*, toasts were raised to the new parents, the twins, Charlotte's health, and anything else they could think of to keep the wine flowing.

~

Today, their guests had departed and although both Charlotte and Zacharie were profoundly grateful for everything they had done, were also pleased to have their quiet lives back — quiet being a relative concept with two squalling babies in the house.

That evening, once the children — all four of them — had eaten, been bathed, changed, where necessary winded, and in bed, Charlotte and Zacharie were alone in the library. Half-reclining on the chaise, Charlotte was curled up against her husband, her head cushioned on his chest. Zacharie had his arm around his wife, pinning her to his side, his fingers trailing absently up and down her shoulder.

"What are you thinking about," Zacharie broke the comfortable peace to ask.

"Fate," came the succinct reply.

"And what does she have in store now? Can you discern her intent?"

Charlotte, hearing amusement in her husband's voice, nudged him in the shoulder. "You may mock, but I was just thinking of the curious path we both followed to get here and that with a single change of direction we would never have met."

There was a long silence.

"Ahhh… but that is the thing about Fate, *ma chérie.*" Zacharie smiled. "If she has a plan, however curious and convoluted it might seem, she will always ensure it comes to fruition. That is why she is named Fate, and who are we, mere mortals, to argue? I, for one, am eternally thankful she chose to interfere in my humdrum life and send me to you."

"And I am endlessly glad she did. You made me want to live again, before ever I realised you had stolen my heart.

"*Mon amour,*" Zacharie's voice lowered to a sensual growl.

"*Mon cœur…*" the longing in Charlotte's whispered reply was unmistakable.

Of one mind, and in a rustle of silks, they tumbled off the chaise onto the luxurious rug in front of the blazing fire.

While Zacharie affirmed his love for Charlotte in *the* most ardent manner, Fate smiled and brushed her hands together.

Mission accomplished.

~

The Daffodil Garden

His Fiery Hoyden - A Regency Novella
A Regency Duet
A Regency Christmas Double

<u>Contemporary Romances</u>
Of Ruins and Romance
All At Once It's You
Cobweb Dreams

<u>Anthologies</u>
The Lady's Wager - For Melissa
Love Kindled - Building Love
Winning Emma - With Love From London - Voyages of the
Heart: Vol 1

The Pomegranate Tree
Hannah's Heirloom - Book One

Hoping to trace the origins of an ancient ruby clasp, a gift from her long dead grandmother, Hannah Wilson travels to the fortress of Masada with her best friend, Max. Strange dreams concerning a rebel ambush begin to haunt Hannah and following a tragic accident, she slips into the world of Ancient Masada.

A woman out of time, Hannah must rely on her instincts and her knowledge of what will befall this citadel to survive. Will she escape, or is she doomed to die along with hundreds of others as Masada falls – and what does any of this have to do with an ancient ruby clasp?

Echoes of Stone and Fire
Hannah's Heirloom - Book Two

Pompeii - a vibrant city lost in time following the AD79 eruption of Vesuvius. Now rediscovered, archaeologists yearn for an opportunity to uncover the town's past. Some things, however, are best left alone - revealing the secrets hidden beneath the stones could prove perilous. Hannah and Max are brought to Pompeii by a surprise invitation to join an excavation team who are trying to uncover the city's long history.

After entering an excavated house that bears a Hebrew inscription, Hannah's two worlds collide, and she falls back through time to ancient Pompeii. A place where her ancestor is a physician to gladiators engaged in mortal combat, where riotous mobs run amok and where a ghost from the past returns to haunt her.

Will Hannah and her loved ones manage to escape the devastation she knows is coming, before the town is engulfed in volcanic ash? Will she ever find her way back to Max the love of her life, waiting not so patiently millennia away? Or will echoes be all that remain?

Embers of Destiny
Hannah's Heirloom - Book Three

AD80 - Hannah and Maxentius must embark on a new journey to Northern Britannia. This harsh frontier is far from the comforts of Rome and danger lurks where least expected; a garrison of soldiers, some unhappy with their isolated posting; local tribes, outwardly accepting of their Roman occupier, but who may still resent the seizure of their lands.

Millennia away, Hannah Vallier finds a familiar item while working in a museum near Hadrian's Wall. It is the pomegranate; carved by Maxentius on Masada. Before Hannah can discuss it with Max, disaster strikes! Believing her husband has been killed, Hannah retreats into the past, her soul melding with that of her ancestor, but with little idea of what they could face. Is the risk from the conquered tribes, or much closer to home?

As rebellion threatens to shatter a fragile peace, Hannah's heart whispers that just maybe Max isn't dead and that he is calling her home. Can she trust her heart, or will she remain caught out of time, her destiny floating away like embers on a breeze?

Etched in Starlight
Hannah's Heirloom - Prequel

Maxentius - a Roman soldier fresh from the battlefields of Armenia, arrives to take command of the military outpost of Masada, Herod's isolated citadel in the Judaean desert. A seemingly mundane posting after years of warfare, Maxentius finds it more challenging to maintain a focused garrison than to face the wrath of the Parthians across a disputed frontier.

Hannah - a young Hebrew physician spends her days dealing with injuries from street brawls, deprivation, disease and loss. As her beloved Jerusalem plunges into chaos; her brother — who belongs to a band of rebels determined to drive out their Roman occupiers — tells her of their plans to storm a desert fortress and steal the weapons stored there, persuading his reluctant sister to go with him.

Masada - following the ambush, Hannah finds and treats three badly wounded Roman soldiers. In the aftermath and against impossible odds, Hannah and Maxentius realise that they are more than healer and captive, their fate already etched in starlight.

Prelude to Fate

For Lucia, staring into the jaws of an horrific death, escape seems impossible.

Rufius Atellus, a veteran Roman soldier, is appalled when he recognises one of the victims about to be executed. Surely this is a ghastly mistake?

A ferocious she-wolf, anticipating a tasty meal, suddenly finds herself under a human's control.

In an unexpected twist, and as danger threatens, the lives of all three become inextricably entwined.

Was it chance brought them together in that theatre of bloodshed, or simply a prelude to fate?

Once Upon An Earl
A Regency Romance
Linen and Lace - Book One

When Fate saw fit to intervene in the life of Giles Trevallier, the very respectable Earl of Winchester, by dropping a female — soaked to the skin and with no memory of who she is or how she came to be there — literally at his feet, no one could have predicted the outcome.

While uncovering her identity, Giles realises he is falling hopelessly in love with his mystery guest, who unbeknownst to him, is succumbing to similar emotions; but, when the heart is involved, a thoughtless word or gesture can thwart even Fate's best-laid plans.

Faced with misunderstandings, whispers of scandal, secret documents and foreign agents, their chance at a happy ever after seems elusive, but fairy tales often happen when least expected, and love — however inconvenient — usually finds a way to conquer all.

To Unlock Her Heart

A Regency Romance
Linen and Lace - Book Two

Abused by a duke, and shunned by Society, relief seems at hand when Grace Aldeburgh is bequeathed a house in a small village, far from malicious gossips.

Once there, a tentative friendship blooms between Grace and Theo Elliott, the local doctor, who has already resolved to be the man to unlock her heart.

Just when happiness appears to be within her grasp, her erstwhile tormentor once again stalks Grace. After a failed kidnap attempt, the duke's quest culminates in an acrimonious confrontation, and the reason for his venal pursuit becomes agonisingly clear.

Love on a Winter's Tide
A Regency Romance
Linen and Lace - Book Three

Every day, Helena disappears into a world few acknowledge, helping the poor, downtrodden, and abused. A husband is the last thing she can be bothered with.

Busy managing his shipping line, Hugh Drummond sees no need for a wife, whose only joy is dancing and frivolity. If — and it was a huge if — he ever married, it would be to a woman as capable as he, not some giddy society Miss.

Then, Hugh meets Helena and despite their resolve, fate, it seems, has other ideas. As their attraction deepens however, treachery threatens to tear them apart. Will they uncover the perpetrator in time, or will their love be swept away, lost forever on a winter's tide?

A Love Unquenchable
A Regency Romance
Linen and Lace - Book Four

Jessica Drummond, a bright and cheerful young woman, rarely gives romance, let alone love, a thought. Long hours working in her brother's shipping office affords little chance of her ever meeting an eligible bachelor.

Duncan Barrington, veteran of the Napoleonic Wars, believes himself wounded in both body and soul. He has no intention of inflicting his demons on anyone, certainly not a beautiful and, in his opinion, irresponsible city lady.

One cold and snowy morning, the plight of a bedraggled puppy throws Jessica and Duncan together and, as a spark of something indefinable yet wholly unquenchable begins to burn, it is unclear who rescued whom.

A Hidden Rose
A Regency Romance
Linen and Lace - Book Five

After witnessing his mother's grief at the loss of his father, Nick Drummond resolved never to cause someone he loved such distress. Even the happiness of his siblings would not sway him – until he met Rose.

Rose Archer was almost content assisting her doctor father in a tiny fishing village in the north of Yorkshire. To experience the world beyond, a tantalising dream – until she met Nick.

Unexpectedly, the impossible becomes possible, and the renounced – desired above all things, but the shipwreck that brought them together, may yet tear them apart. Will Nick learn to trust his heart, or will his love for Rose remain forever hidden?

The Daffodil Garden
A Regency Romance

Horrifically scarred during the war, William Harcourt - Marquis of Blackthorne - prefers to spend his days in the quiet of his daffodil garden; plants do not pity, turn away, or judge.

Lucy Truscott, whose life is far removed from that of the *ton*, has no idea that by saving the life of a young woman, to whom she bears an uncanny resemblance, her own will be placed in mortal danger.

A chance encounter leads to something more. William begins to trust that Lucy sees the man beneath the scars, while Lucy is persuaded that love might actually transcend status.

Unfortunately, before their courtship has really begun, someone has every intention of ending it - permanently.

His Fiery Hoyden
A Regency Novella

Please inform your master, Sasha is perfectly happy here with me and there is more chance of hell freezing over, than of my brother dancing attendance on his Grace."

A plea for help ignored. A child left to bring up her baby brother.

Livvy has no respect for the nobility; they let her down when she most needed them. Why should she accede to their demands now?

Philip, Lord Harrington, is stunned to discover the young heir to the dukedom lives a stone's throw away in a ramshackle cottage, and resolves to restore the child to his birthright.

They meet in a clash of wills, but just when it seems Livvy might surrender, the victory Philip desires, may not taste all that sweet.

A REGENCY DUET

Luck be a Pirate
(first published in the Kiss My Luck Anthology)

Luck wasn't something retired pirate Kennet Alexson believed in
– good or bad. However, even he had to concede that landing a
job at Trentams shipyard, and meeting Lynette Collins, was more
than coincidence.

Fortune it seemed, was smiling on him for once.

As Kennet adjusts to life on dry land, his friendship with
Lynette deepens into something far more enduring, and what
once seemed elusive now becomes possible.

Unfortunately, fate has other plans, and Kennet's good luck is
about to run out.

The Highwayman's Kiss
(first published in the Once Upon a Love anthology)

Nothing exciting had ever happened to Juliette St Clair. Her days
were spent assisting her father or calling on friends, wandering
art galleries, taking constitutionals or, and more preferably,

escaping into her books. Her evenings her evenings — an endless round of balls, where she preferred to remain invisible.

Until the day she was robbed by a highwayman.

A REGENCY CHRISTMAS DOUBLE

Heart Rescued
(first published in the Tales for the Season Anthology)

Four years since Jasper lost the woman he was hoping to marry. Four years since he closed his heart and withdrew from Society. He has no idea his reclusive existence is about to be shattered.

Enter his sister's best friend, Harriet, a flame haired beauty, who needs his help.

Reluctantly he agrees and as they spend time together, it is clear their feelings run deep. Although Harriet affects Jasper in a way no woman ever has, he believes her to be out of his league ~ but it's Christmas and she might just be the one to melt his frozen heart

Catch a Snowflake

Romance often blossoms in the most unlikely of places - but in a ward full of wounded soldiers - surely not?

When Lucas Withers comes face to face with Jemima Parsons - a young woman who blames him for her brother's injury -

falling in love is the last thing on their minds. What neither of them anticipated, was the magic of snowflakes.

CONTEMPORARY ROMANCE

Of Ruins and Romance

While escorting a group of tourists around the ancient Roman port of Ostia, Kassandra Winters bumps into someone she first met in less than auspicious circumstances two years previously. The encounter leads to a job offer - to be the assistant guide for a three-week tour of ancient sites in and around Rome. Unable to resist such an opportunity, Kassie agrees.

Kassie has intrigued Gabriel St Germain since he accidentally knocked her flying outside her university professor's office. Her face haunts his dreams, yet he never expected to see her again. So, he is surprised when she appears, as though destined to do so, in the middle of a ruin, and he concocts a plan to win her heart.

Gabriel's old-fashioned courtship touches something deep inside Kassie and, although struggling to believe someone as handsome as Gabriel could possibly be interested in her, she soon realises she has fallen irrevocably in love with him. However, just as Kassie shares everything of herself with Gabriel, her world comes crashing down. Can their romance survive, or will it fall in ruins, like the relics of antiquity that brought them together?

All At Once It's You

When Alex arrives in the small village of Rosedale Abbey, to take up a position as a research assistant for a renowned archaeologist, the last thing she is looking for, or expects to find, is love.

Jake was perfectly happy with the status quo. When it came to relationships, he didn't do committed or long term. He called the shots, and if his current flame didn't like it, she knew what to do. A philosophy, which served him well - until he met Alex.

Romance blooms, but even as the untamed wilderness of the North Yorkshire moors weaves its spell, a long-buried secret might yet jeopardise their happily ever after.

Cobweb Dreams
A Novella

A holiday on the Scottish isle of Mull was just the break Chloe Shepherd needed, an escape from her boring office job and her complete lack of anything resembling a social life. Romance, it seems, isn't on the cards and, although Chloe dreams of finding her soulmate she is beginning to believe love is like cobwebs — spun overnight, only to vanish in the early morning breeze.

Under sufferance, Dominic Winters makes a flying visit to Mull to check on a rental property owned by his family. He hasn't got time for this — so indulging in a holiday fling is the last thing on his mind.

A lamb stuck in a bog proves a most unexpected matchmaker and, while Mull weaves its magic, Chloe wonders whether those fragile cobwebs might be far more stubborn than she thought.

www.ingramcontent.com/pod-product-compliance
Lightning Source LLC
Chambersburg PA
CBHW071530100726
47908CB00004B/1353